Table of Contents

The Vicar's Frozen Heart

The Hornsby Brothers #2

By

Karyn Gerrard

The Vicar's Frozen Heart
Copyright © 2016, 2020 by Karyn Gerrard
KG Publishing
Vers 2.1
PRINT ISBN: 978-1-7386845-4-0
Cover art by © The Write Designer

The Hornsby Brothers Series

THREE BROTHERS, THE sons of the Duke of Gransford, are diverse in their natures, and so too, are their choices when it comes to love. Growing up in an affectionate household, each is determined to hold out for true love. Searching for it, however, is different from finding— and leads each of the brothers to unlikely places and chance encounters with what society would consider unsuitable women.

BOOK ONE IS *Bold Seduction (of Professor Hornsby)* and concerns the youngest son, Spencer Hornsby.

Book two is *The Vicar's Frozen Heart* and concerns the middle son, Tremain Hornsby.

Book three is *The Marquess of Secrets* and concerns the oldest son and heir to the duke, Harrison Hornsby, the Marquess of Tennington.

Author's Note

THE VICAR'S FROZEN Heart was previously published with Kensington/Lyrical Press. This revised version is copyrighted in 2020.

Tremain has PTSD (Post Traumatic Stress Disorder), although it was not recognized as such in the Victorian era. With soldiers, it was called 'hysteria' in the Victorian age. By WW I: 'shell shock.' WW II: 'combat fatigue.' People suffered from this for hundreds, even thousands of years, but it wasn't until the 1980s that doctors gave it a formal diagnosis.

I should clarify about the youngest Hornsby brother, Spencer. (Book #1 Bold Seduction (of Professor Hornsby) If diagnosed today, Spencer would fall on the spectrum of a mild form of autism. In the Victorian era, there were recorded accounts of children manifesting similar aspects. Back then, they were usually diagnosed with 'children's psychosis' and taken to the asylum.

Summary

HIS HEART NEEDS TO heal.

He sheltered her from the storm and nursed her back to health. But Tremain Hornsby is more than just a village vicar performing a chivalrous duty. He's an ex-soldier ravaged by war, the second son of a duke living under another name, hiding his aristocratic heritage. Yet, despite his secrets, he cannot help but be drawn to the fallen beauty and asks her to stay and care for the orphan in his charge.

AND HERS IS LOST.

Society has deemed Eliza Winston a disgraced governess. Dismissed, robbed, and left to perish, she finds herself in Tremain's home—and soon realizes her handsome rescuer is the one in need of healing. Though a daunting task, Eliza is determined to thaw the vicar's frozen heart—but her own is in danger. Tremain is not only the man she dreamed of but a nobleman—making him an impossible match.

Chapter 1

DURING HER SHORT LIFE, Eliza Winston had been reprimanded more than once for her bluntness and impulsive actions. Still, she'd never experienced a dressing down quite as vicious as the one Lady Bowater was giving her. Standing in the drawing room with the housekeeper, Mrs. Travers, Eliza faced the firing squad with her head held high. But inside? Her emotions were in turmoil.

"I will not tolerate this sort of loose morals in any member of my staff, Miss Winston. Especially *not* in a governess," Lady Bowater huffed. "Do you deny you've had carnal relations with my son?"

"I do not deny it. If you ask William, my lady, he will inform you that the consensual assignation was brief." Eliza's voice shook at the last words.

Their affair had lasted ten days, culminating with two mediocre tumbles between the sheets. Well, perhaps more than passable, as Eliza had limited experience. None at all if the truth were told.

"He's Mr. Winters to you, my girl!" Mrs. Travers snapped.

Lady Bowater held up her hand to silence the housekeeper. "I've spoken with my son, and he claims that he's formed an attachment to you. It will not be borne. He's agreed that the time has come for a stint

7

in the army. It will do him a world of good. Build character. Quite a shame we cannot do the same with you."

Eliza winced inwardly.

Poor William.

"You've worked here two years, and I am extremely disappointed that my trust in you has been sorely misplaced. I am dismissing you effective immediately." Mrs. Travers bobbed her head in agreement at Lady Bowater's admonishing tone. "I will give you twenty pounds, but I *will* have assurances you will not turn up on this doorstep again, even if you find yourself with child. Those are the conditions."

It sounded as if Lady Bowater had done this before. Eliza would not be surprised as William had two older brothers.

Wait. Twenty pounds? A year's wages?

The large amount was to ensure that she would keep quiet in case there were consequences to the liaison. There would be no child. With knowledge comes power, and Eliza had insisted that William wore sheaths, though there was no guarantee. Notwithstanding, she gave her ladyship a stiff nod in agreement.

Eliza clasped her hands to stem the shaking. Despite her brave front, inside, she was crumbling into pieces. Her heart ached with regret—and shame.

"Mrs. Travers has written you a letter of reference. It's adequate for your needs." The housekeeper thrust an envelope into Eliza's hand. "Your trunk has been packed and brought downstairs. Furthermore, I've arranged transport to take you far from this estate and Yorkshire."

"My lady, why provide transportation?" Eliza didn't like the sound of this. "A carriage ride to the nearest train would be tolerable enough."

Lady Bowater took a step toward her. "I want you off the property immediately. If you are waiting about for the trains, William could find you. He is young and impulsive."

Goodness, Lady Bowater was not wasting a moment. It indeed appeared as if she'd done this before. Undoubtedly, there were many scenes with the older sons over the years.

"It's seven o'clock, my lady. Couldn't my departure wait until morning?" Eliza asked, her voice shaking on the last two words as the reality of what was happening took hold.

"No. For the exact motive I've stated. There is to be no further contact between you and my son. I want you gone—before he discovers your absence. There's been enough drama for my liking."

Lady Bowater handed an envelope to Mrs. Travers, who in turn passed it to Eliza, repulsion evident on both their faces. Eliza's heart tumbled, the ramifications of her brief dalliance hitting hard. She had managed to secure a good position through sheer determination. And now? Ruined.

All on me.

What a colossal blunder. Eliza ruined herself because she showed no forbearance in the face of a tempting rendezvous. She was more intelligent than that. At least, Eliza had thought so. All she had to do was say no. Be strong and resolute.

"My men will escort you through the night to Dover. The farther you are from here, the better."

"Dover?" Eliza blinked rapidly. "My lady, wouldn't travel by train the entire distance be more expedient?"

"I don't trust you. You could disembark at any stop. I want you delivered personally to the Southeast Coast," Lady Bowater answered haughtily. "However, I gave my men permission to use the train part of the way should the weather deteriorate."

Eliza gulped. "But I've never been to Southeast England. I don't know anyone—"

"Exactly. Begone from my sight. Vixen." Lady Bowater's face flushed with self-righteous anger or abhorrence, maybe both, as Eliza couldn't be sure—dramatic words from a woman who claimed to despise drama.

It sounds like a line from an overwrought play.

Eliza wasn't sure whether to laugh or cry.

Lady Bowater's eyes narrowed. "Seducer of innocent boys."

Boy?

Granted, pretty William was four years her junior, but he was certainly old enough for an illicit encounter at twenty years of age. And hardly all that innocent, as he appeared to know what he was about in bed. Nevertheless, the words hit their mark, churning her insides.

Mrs. Travers clasped Eliza's elbow tightly and steered her from the room. "A fine mess you've got yourself in, my girl. All to have a young lordling in your bed. Stupid, stupid," Mrs. Travers whispered as she pulled her toward the downstairs entrance.

She wriggled out of the housekeeper's clutches. "One moment, please. Allow me to inspect my room one last time and collect my coat and reticule. At least grant me that."

Sighing, Mrs. Travers did an about-face and pulled Eliza upstairs toward the servants' quarters. For an older lady, she could move quickly. An enormous ring of keys bounced against her hip with each long stride. Mrs. Travers stopped in front of the door and released her. Frowning, Eliza rubbed her arm. Thanks to the housekeeper's tight grip, there will no doubt be bruises.

"Make haste," Mrs. Travers ordered. "I'll wait here."

After slipping into the room, Eliza closed the door and leaned against it. Tears welled in her eyes the instant she found herself alone.

What have I done?

She'd made a complete muck of things. With no family to turn to, what could she do?

Dover. Good heavens.

She didn't have to stay in the immediate vicinity; she could travel anywhere with twenty pounds. The money and reference would be lost if she refused to follow Lady Bowater's demand. It would be best to make a swift and quiet exit. Perhaps a fresh start on the opposite end of the country *was* prudent.

Blinking away the tears, she sniffled while glancing about the room. She loved her living space. It was bright and pleasant, with a comfortable bed and a large window to let in the sunlight. Better accommodations than at the orphanage. It had become—home. Or what she imagined home was.

During the past two years, Eliza had added little touches to make the room her own, a rug, a framed picture of a calm ocean, and a blue quilt with a star design. The items weren't here; hopefully, they were placed in her trunk and not tossed in the rubbish bin. Inspecting all the drawers and seeing that nothing was left behind, Eliza spied her shawl on a wall hook. She pulled it down, opened the envelope, and carefully separated the pound notes, tucking a few in each of the shawl's hidden pockets.

When traveling with money, hiding it on your person was the sensible thing to do. The wool coat must be with her trunk. Standing in the middle of the room, a tug of regret filled her; how she would miss Lady Susanna, her delightful young charge. They wouldn't even allow her to say goodbye.

A right mess, indeed.

Curiosity and a spark of passion caused her to throw away her hard-won position and security.

Eliza grew up at the St. Ann's Industrial School and Orphanage and studied to be a governess, a respected position within the pecking order of the servant world. Not an easy situation to obtain, but she had accomplished it. Only to abandon it as soon as William's lips touched hers. Perhaps she *was* a vixen. No, she was lonely and had been her whole life. That is why she tossed all common sense to the wind.

Too late for regrets.

This sorry situation called for showing a brave face. Eliza would depart this estate as calmly as she could. Like it or not, it was time to move on with the rest of her life.

ELIZA COULD NOT SAY how many hours had passed. The rocking of the carriage made sleep impossible. Instead, she recalled the humiliating scolding she'd received. How arrogant of her to think she could indulge in a clandestine relationship with the earl's youngest son. His handsome face, golden hair, and broad shoulders awakened something inside her. A passion she had no inkling existed.

Such intimacy.

Perhaps William sensed her desperation for warmth and human contact. Somehow, she doubted the young man was aware of another's loneliness.

Rubbing her burning, tired eyes, Eliza pushed aside the curtain and glanced outside. Complete blackness filled the horizon except for the snow tumbling from the sky. The snow looked to be rather deep. Considering it was the middle of January, a clear road for passage was too much to ask. With a sudden jolt, the carriage came to a halt.

One of the men clamored down and opened the door. "'Tis cold ridin' up there. Thought I'd get a wee bit of warmth from ye, lassie."

Even in dark shadows, Eliza could see the lascivious look on the older man's face. In this, she was not mistaken.

Oh, no.

"Where are we? What's the time—wait, what are you doing?" Eliza cried.

He pushed into the carriage, slammed the door, and banged on the roof. The carriage lurched forward, slowly at first, as if struggling to move through the snow. Unpleasant sweat, whiskey, and cheap pipe tobacco odors filled the interior. A horrible scar pulled the man's mouth into a sadistic leer.

"I searched your trunk up top. No money. Give over, lass. Where 'tis it? Don't be lyin' to me. I heard the whole sorry tale in the servant's dinin' hall. I know the old hag gave ye money." He snatched the reticule from her wrist with a rough tug, snapping the straps. He looked inside, frowned, and tossed it to the floor. Grunting, he pushed her down and lay on top of her, his large hands running up and down her body. Then he crammed them in her coat, searching her pockets.

Eliza shuddered with horror when the man's growing erection pressed against her thigh.

"Give it over, or I'll take the amount out of your cunny. His young lordship left ye well oiled; I'll be bound," he hissed in her ear. "You're not the first nor the last. Those Winter boys like their fun. They won't mind if I take their leavings."

A hand closed about her throat, the callous tips of his fingers scraping her skin. Scar leaned in, his foul breath turning her stomach. "Give it to me, or I'll hump the truth from ye." His other hand fumbled with the fall of his trousers.

No. No. No!

Frantically, Eliza pulled off one of her wool gloves with her teeth, then raked her nails over his eye and down his cheek. Scar screamed, releasing his hold. Scrambling backward, he buried his face in his hands, droplets of blood oozing between his meaty fingers.

The driver must have heard his partner's screech, for the carriage slowed slightly. Turning, she fumbled with the door handle.

Escape!

Eliza's heart banged against her ribs at a frightening pace. Scar recovered quickly, grabbing her arm and wrenching her shoulder, then he smashed his clenched fist into her face. Bone cracked, and blood trickled over her lips.

A jolt of intense pain spiraled through her, causing her vision to blur, but she finally grasped the handle and gave it a turn, causing the door to fling open wide. The carriage was still moving.

Jump!

What choice did she have? About to lunge forward, Scar caught a fistful of her shawl and pulled her back in. Blindly she fought him. Her breathing labored, landing blows where she could. He swore obscenely and shook her hard. In the fracas, her shawl came off.

The money!

Eliza desperately grabbed it, but Scar shoved her, and she tumbled backward out of the swaying carriage. Hitting the ground hard, she rolled and rolled, gathering cold snow until she came to a halt in a ditch. Searing pain covered her entire body.

"Whoa, there!" the driver called out. Drifting in and out of consciousness, she heard snippets of conversation and raised voices wafting in the cold night air.

"What did ye do, ye great lummox! Ye were to get the money, nothing else."

"Bitch fought me. She rolled down a hill, probably dead."

"Be damned if I be checking. It was an accident, not our fault. Her ladyship never needs to know. Not that she'd care much. Throw the trunk off and—"

"Look, here 'tis. Hidden in her shawl. Aye, let's ditch the trunk and head to London. I could do with a pint and a slice of kidney pie."

Eliza heard more chatter sprinkled with smug laughter. They were going to leave her here to freeze to death. Eliza lay perfectly still in case they returned to do further investigating. Satisfied with finding the money—*oh, my money*—she heard the trunk hit the ground with a decided thud. With a snap of the reins, the men drove off.

Snowflakes gathered on her lashes. Could she stand? No. Instead, Eliza tried to crawl. Could it be a house she'd spotted amongst the trees, or was her scrambled mind playing tricks? Tasting blood, she pulled herself through the snow. A white-hot stab of pain shot through her head, and everything turned black.

Chapter 2

SINCE SWEARING OFF laudanum, Tremain Colson had become a fitful sleeper. The incessant pain in his leg often woke him several times during the night. After lighting the wick in the oil lamp beside his bed, he glanced at the wall clock at half past four.

What sort of racket awoke him? The whinny of horses—and men's voices raised in excitement and anger. What brain-addled individuals would be traveling this time of night and in inclement weather? There was also a loud thump, like a person had tossed something heavy to the ground.

The temptation to roll over and ignore the clamor had crossed his mind, but something kept nudging him to investigate. That thudding sound could be a human, and no one could survive long in these stormy conditions.

With an exasperated sigh, Tremain swung his legs around the side of the bed and sat upright, rubbing his eyes and grunting at the pang that shot up his right limb. He pushed himself into a standing position, then limped to his small wardrobe and dressed swiftly. Clasping his cane, Tremain ventured into the darkened hallway, located a lamp, and lit it. After slipping on his wool greatcoat and gloves, he wrapped a thick scarf around his head and face, then headed outside. A blast of icy wind slammed into him, seizing his breath.

Holding the light aloft, Tremain cautiously ventured across his property. A large trunk lay in a drift of snow. The deep ruts left behind by a carriage were already filling in. Snow swirled all about him as the wind howled with a woeful wail. Turning in a circle, he looked about. Nothing but white as far as the eye could see. And dark sky. His gaze skirted across a large mound. There in the ditch, a bare hand lay exposed.

Tremain tottered toward the trench, taking his time as the ground inclined downward. Sitting the lantern and his cane at his feet, he swiped away the loose snow.

An unconscious woman.

Blood covered the lower part of her face. At that moment, a gust of wind blew out the lantern, and complete darkness surrounded him. Good thing he knew his way about the property and the woods beyond. He'd have to carry her, and her weight would place ungodly pressure on his mangled leg, but he could not do much else under the circumstances.

With great effort, Tremain managed to slip the woman over his shoulder. His right leg turned numb when he tried to straighten it, and it started to buckle under him. He went down like a sack of potatoes yet kept his grip on the young lady.

Taking several deep breaths, then exhaling forcefully, he tried again and stood on his feet after a couple of attempts. To hell with the lantern. He'd fetch it later. Same with the trunk and his cane. With great care, he made his way toward his residence, carried the lady to his room, then collapsed on his bed with a great groan. Tremain landed on top of her, but the woman didn't stir. Out of breath, he sat back, taking in the vision before him.

A female in his bed. How long had it been? More than three years.

The young woman was certainly attractive enough. Leave it to him to have amorous thoughts. Tremain removed her bonnet, and golden curls spilled into his hands. Her hairstyle was askew, pins hanging from the luxuriant locks. Unbuttoning her wool coat, he nearly groaned at the ample curves evident even with her shapeless gray skirt and the starched blouse buttoned to her neck.

Don't focus on the young woman's looks. Assist her.

Tremain collected a basin of warm water and a cloth, then wiped away the dried, frozen blood. Bruises were already visible, and her nose appeared broken. Someone had punched her square in the face. Beaten, perhaps robbed—or worse—and left to perish in the snow.

At least the perpetrator had not torn her garments. Perhaps there was no violation. Her chest rose and fell, proof she still lived. There's a mercy.

Once he built up the fire, Tremain retrieved his cane, dragged the trunk inside, then located his first aid kit and a flask of brandy. Already exhaustion covered him, and it was an effort to even walk to his room. Due to his past stint in the army, he could tend to superficial injuries, and he did so here by placing plasters on her facial cuts. With a gentle slide of his fingers, he reset the bone in her nose. A partial break. She was lucky. It would not mare her looks.

The lady stirred, moaning slightly, but didn't regain consciousness. So Tremain elevated her head with an extra pillow and opened her blouse's first few buttons to make her more comfortable. What to do? Grabbing his cane, he hobbled to the front entrance and stepped outside the door. Icicles hung from the roof, and he reached for one, breaking it free before smashing it and wrapping the pieces in a cloth.

Returning to his bedroom, Tremain sat by the bed, holding the icepack to her nose. The noticeable swelling dissipated. What should he do next? Remove the wet clothes? She would catch a chill if he didn't.

A strange mixture of anticipation and dread spread through him. It's not as if he possessed anything as fundamental as human feelings or desires. Not any longer. Tremain would approach this detached and calculatedly as he did everything else in his life of late.

Despite his best effort to remain impersonal, he responded to the lovely vision before him. He cursed inwardly at his lack of control, deciding to ignore it and complete the task at hand. Tremain stripped her to her shift.

He slumped into the chair once he covered her with two woolen blankets and a quilt since her skin was chilly to the touch. The young lady's figure was lush, her curves soft, just as he liked it.

I used to like it.

What was going to do with her?

The storm could continue for another day—or more. In the nearby village of Hawksgreen, one of the local farmers had predicted this storm by the direction of his weathervane and his trusty Farmer's Almanac. Considering the man was never wrong, Tremain had stocked up with extra food—a decidedly prudent move since there was an unexpected—and for the most part—unwanted guest.

Tremain frowned. Company was the last thing he wanted. He had been looking forward to the solitude for however long the storm lasted. To be free from duty and service for forty-eight hours was a pleasant prospect.

Exhaling, he slanted his glance at the clock: close to six. The sun would be rising soon, no more sleep as he was wide awake. Reaching for the flask of brandy on the table, he took a deep drink, allowing the comforting, slow burn to curl down his throat.

And how would he, of all people, explain the presence of a woman in his residence? Especially a golden-haired lady with a siren's body and no doubt cornflower blue eyes. The situation should prove interesting if nothing else—no two ways about it. When the weather broke, she could not linger regardless of her injuries.

Tremain watched her. And would continue to do so until she awoke. As soon as the storm dissipated, he would see her on her way. Then he could return to his self-imposed, semi-isolated life.

SEARING PAIN.

That was the first sensation Eliza experienced as the hazy fog cleared from her mind. Blinking, she tried to focus. Clutching a fistful of a wool blanket, she concluded that she lay in a bed.

Oh, thank God.

Who had rescued her? So, it *was* a house she'd seen through the trees. Eliza tried to raise her head and lift her arms, but no luck. No sitting upright for her. Not yet. Instead, she glanced about the room. It was a man's private lair, as evidenced by the dark wood walls and green and brown colors of the curtains and bedding. On one wall was a tall bookcase.

In the hearth, a fire crackled, and off to the side stood an oversized, overstuffed chair. A pair of silver spectacles lay on a table nearby, and a black waistcoat hung on a hook. Perhaps a kindly, older man had come to her rescue, considering the books, glasses, and plain clothing—a grandfatherly type with balding white hair and apple cheeks who would take pity on her calamitous situation.

She brought the blanket to her nose and sniffed—a faintly spicy, masculine scent that was not unpleasant. Eliza's entire body throbbed with pain. The fall from the carriage no doubt had done some damage.

The door swung open and banged against the wall, startling her. A tall, imposing man, leaning heavily on a cane, crossed the threshold. Dressed entirely in black, he hobbled closer to the bed. What an austere face. On either side of his mouth were etched deep frown lines. He scowled at her.

Here stood a man the furthest thing from a kind grandfather. He was handsome, she supposed, a man of thirty-odd years, with his raven-black hair and sculpted cheekbones, but his chilly expression evoked no warmth at all. His silver-gray eyes held the shade of chips of ice. Much like a stern schoolmaster or unforgiving, sober priest, both of which Eliza had enough of in her life.

"You're awake then?" The words were clipped and precise.

"T-t-thank you, sir," she croaked. "Your name?"

The cane thumped heavily on the floor as he made his way to stand at her bedside. "Tremain Colson."

A deep voice, but it held no cordiality at all. Well, Eliza was thankful that he found her and took her in. However, she would be out on her backside as soon as she became mobile. "My trunk?"

"I've recovered it. It's there." Mr. Colson pointed to the opposite side of the room. "I found you at half past four this morning. It's now three in the afternoon."

Goodness.

She'd slept around the clock. Eliza lifted the blankets and peered under them.

I'm only wearing my shift.

Did this iceberg of a man strip off her garments? Good heavens, did he lay his hands on her? The memory of that horrid man in the carriage caused her to shudder.

"My clothes?" she croaked.

"I hung them by the fire in the parlor. May I have your name?"

"Eliza. Eliza Winston. Where am I?"

"The village of Hawksgreen. Where were you heading?"

The fright she'd initially experienced dissipated, even though he continued to act in a grave, unfriendly manner. What a dark, brooding man. He had quite the presence.

"Dover—I think."

"Are you in pain?"

She gave him a brisk nod in reply.

"I will make you a cup of willow bark tea." He turned on his heel and hobbled out. Eliza could not help but admire the view. Well-proportioned with broad shoulders. The clothes fit him well; the coat hugged a slim waist.

Had Mr. Colson injured his leg during her rescue, or was it a more permanent state? He certainly grimaced in pain as he turned to leave. Considering his disability, how surprising that he was able to bring her and her trunk into his home. It explained his cross look. He could be suffering much discomfort.

Where was Hawksgreen? A shiver of apprehension ran along her spine. She must construct a sound plan for her future, a strategy that was all the harder to make since the robbery. Not a farthing to her name, and she possessed nothing of value to sell. Eliza doubted this man would be empathetic to her plight. Perhaps he had a long-suffering, kindly wife who would take pity on her. If she must exaggerate her injuries slightly to gain more time, she would.

A horrible prospect, and not like her at all. Eliza couldn't abide by any form of deceit. But one must adapt to one's situation.

And hers was dire.

Chapter 3

MISS WINSTON'S EYES were *not* blue but sparkling green as polished emeralds. When she'd met his gaze, his insides had tumbled with yearning. Dismissing his inappropriate response, he continued into the kitchen, pain tearing from his right thigh to his knee like a hundred sharpened knives sliced into muscle and bone.

Tremain was undoubtedly paying the price for his nocturnal adventure. If he possessed an ounce of common sense, he would sit by the fire, his leg resting on the stool, sipping brandy and reading. Instead, he hobbled about waiting on a stranger—a woman.

A very attractive woman.

When the swelling and redness dissipated, her true beauty would be evident. Lighting the stove and turning up the flame, Tremain shook his head. It appeared he was lonelier than he initially believed. Huffing with frustration, Tremain filled the kettle and set it on the burner.

First order of business: discover Miss Winston's story, and make immediate arrangements to see her from the premises. If he believed in fate—which he did not—he would wonder why and for what purpose such a striking woman wound up on his property. To shake up his staid life? Tempt him into lascivious thoughts and actions long forgotten and buried?

The storm still raged outside. Tremain could not toss her out in it, but be damned if he would allow a storm to start brewing inside of him.

Tremain made the tea and a cup for himself to ease the insistent, throbbing ache in his leg, then carefully carried them to his bedroom, his cane tucked under his arm. Miss Winston sat upright, staring out the window at the swirling, blowing snow.

"Quite the storm," she whispered.

"Yes. Though last night was worse."

He held out the steaming mug, and she took it, giving him a brief but shaky smile. Tremain sat next to the bed, wincing as he adjusted his leg.

She took a sip, glancing at him over the rim. "Am I far from Dover?"

"Far enough. You will have to take the public coach to Ashford to catch the train to Dover, which is about an hour and a half's journey. Dover is close to two hours from here, all told. Do you have family there?"

Miss Winston gazed into the murky contents of her cup. "I have no family. And no money. Those wretched men robbed me and—Oh no!" she cried.

"What's wrong?"

"The letter of reference was in my reticule. That horrid man ripped it from my arm and threw it to the floor. No money and no reference. I am certainly in a pickle," she laughed brokenly.

"I think, Miss Winston, you had best tell me your story from the beginning." He placed his cup on the table.

She looked at him, wary and questioning. Green fire flamed in the depth of her eyes. Though vulnerable, there was a steely strength there, too. Tremain found the combination alluring.

"My tale of woe is hardly your concern, Mr. Colson."

"True. But you *will* require my assistance to continue on your journey. You cannot stay here." Tremain winced. His voice was cold and dismissive even to his own ears.

Miss Winston shook her head. "Forgive me. I don't mean to sound ungrateful or rude. I was a governess at Bowater Manor in Ingleton, Yorkshire."

Ah. This occupation explained Miss Wonston's educated tone and proper dress. "You're a long way from Yorkshire."

"Yes. I will speak plainly. The lady of the manor dismissed me from my post for dallying with the youngest son of the Earl of Bowater."

Miss Winston stared at him as if waiting for his censure. Tremain made sure there was no visible reaction to her shocking pronouncement. Instead, he stayed firmly hidden behind his granite mask. He might as well remain silent and allow her to continue.

"I was given twenty pounds along with a mediocre reference, then stuffed in a carriage driven by two men in her ladyship's employ. She instructed them to escort me as far away from Yorkshire as possible. Why she picked Dover, I have no idea."

"There's no possible way you could make it from any place in Yorkshire to Dover in one night, let alone get this far. It's more than two hundred and fifty miles at least."

"I'm telling the truth. We caught a train in Leeds and traveled to London. Once in London, they hired a carriage per her ladyship's plans. We drove all night. The men felt they had journeyed far enough and decided to get rid of me. Does it storm like this often?"

Tremain digested the information. What she explained could be achieved if they journeyed by train most of the way.

Dismissed for a dalliance.

Her tangled, golden locks fell about her shoulders. Though her face was still bruised and swollen, the luminescent pearl shade of her skin shimmered in the firelight. No wonder the son of the house was smitten. It was always the servants who paid the penalty.

By changing the conversation to the weather, it was evident Miss Winston didn't wish to discuss her predicament.

"No. A snowstorm of this magnitude is rare for this part of England." Tremain paused. Though she may be reluctant to discuss it, he had to ask. "Did they harm you? The men, I mean."

"Besides the one brute slamming his fist into my face?" She touched her cheek tentatively and winced. "No. I believe he intended to-to violate me. He said as much. There was a struggle. You see, I hid the money in the secret pockets of my shawl. The beast tore it off me in the melee, the door popped open, and he pushed me out of the moving carriage."

"They left you to perish? Abhorrent."

"Yes, it is. I don't remember much after that. Bits here and there. I think they planned to return to London to celebrate their windfall. And my downfall." She gave him another shaky smile, and his unused heart clenched briefly. "And I cannot believe I confessed all that to you. I am at your mercy, Mr. Colson. I throw myself—at your m-m-mercy." Her voice quivered on the last word.

Not tears. I cannot abide tears.

Tremain rose to his feet. "Try to sleep. We will discuss it further tomorrow," he said as he headed to the door.

Limping into his study, he slammed the door and locked it. He hadn't told Miss Winston yet that he was the vicar of this village. It's not as if he wore his collar around his own house. Suppose he would have to inform her of his vicar status soon enough.

Not that his last name was Colson.

It was actually Hornsby.

The reasons for keeping his true identity secret were a complicated matter. And it was not one he was willing to discuss aloud with anyone, let alone a strange woman in his midst.

Sighing, he rifled through the letters he had picked up at the village yesterday afternoon. A response from his younger brother, Spencer. He would read it soon. He couldn't bring himself to do it quite yet. Recently, he had posted his brother a soul-searching letter. Tremain shouldn't have sent it, for it had revealed far too much.

Tremain remembered every word he'd written:

DEAR SPENCE,

I know you are probably still in Wales, but I sent this to Penhaven because there is no need for a speedy reply, if one at all. But I have to tell of my feelings to someone.

I am not certain I can continue with this. I've become a brooding bastard. It must be bad if even I acknowledge it. And because of it, I've become ineffective with regard to my duties. Perhaps this has all been a mistake. It would be easy to escape to Gransford Manor, but then I remembered what I told you when we were at school. Hold your head high, and don't show fear. I have found it is easier said than done.

I know you are not one for letter writing, but during some break in your research, drop me a line, for I need your sage advice. I am not sure what to do next.

I am lost, Brother.

Love,

Tremain

TREMAIN HORNSBY WAS the middle son of the Duke of Gransford—the broken, crippled, damaged son of the duke. No one here knew of his true identity. Examining the where's and wherefores of his personal mission here was not something he wanted to dwell on. One reason was to heal, inside and out. War can have a way of inflicting damage not clearly visible. He trailed his finger along the corner of his brother's letter. He could not bring himself to read it. Not tonight.

Beyond all that, he could not allow Miss Winston to appeal to him in any way. Never mind that her voluptuous form and golden hair stirred his desire. Yet, her honesty and bravery, mixed with a dose of tremulous vulnerability, managed to chip away a few pieces from the ice-covered wall surrounding his heart. Frustrated, Tremain sat before the fire and stared at the flames until sunset.

ELIZA WOKE TO THE SOUND of a brusque throat clearing. Mr. Colson stood in the doorway holding a tray.

"I brought you something to eat." He walked stiffly toward her as she struggled to sit upright. After laying the tray on her lap, he turned up the lamp and motioned to leave.

"Please, keep me company. If only for a few minutes. Has the storm abated?"

Mr. Colson sat on the chair, looking at everything but her. Had her story disgusted him to such an extent that he could not stand to be in her presence or even meet her gaze?

He crossed his arms. "It's eight in the evening. The snow stopped some hours past."

Eliza inspected the food on the tray—a bowl of beef stew, fresh bread, and cheese. Her mouth watered.

"Did you make this?" she asked.

Mr. Colson shook his head, meeting her gaze briefly. "No. A woman from the village comes in three or four times a week to clean and prepare food. She makes enough to see me through a few meals."

His words, spoken harshly, matched his expression of indifference. No wife or family. No surprise there, as this could very well be the coldest man she'd ever met. How to carry on a conversation with such a human icicle?

"Your words, asking for my mercy," he ventured.

Flushing in mortification, Eliza wished that she could recall them. However, she needed assistance in whatever form. She was not used to asking for aid, so she always made her way in the world. Exaggerating her injuries no longer seemed a wise plan. There would be no fooling this implacable man besides that doing so was distasteful.

"Yes?"

"I will pay for the rest of your journey to Dover."

Oh, thank God.

"If I am to be truthful, I've no desire to travel to Dover," she said matter-of-factly. "I was being escorted there as part of my agreement with Lady Bowater. But seeing both my money and reference are gone, I'm not compelled to journey farther."

"I'm not certain what manner of occupation you can find in a small village such as Hawksgreen. If, as you say, you were a governess—"

"You don't believe me?" she interrupted, her voice rising. "By all means, write to Lady Bowater though I doubt she will reply. Better yet, contact Mrs. Travers, the housekeeper, for she will back up my sorry tale and confirm my previous employment."

Eliza frowned. Though—he didn't know her, and she could not fault him for being cautious. Since Mr. Colson found her beaten and penniless, he had every right to question her account. Remembering the warning that she was not to contact the family, Eliza dismissed that particular codicil because, as far as she was concerned, it was no longer valid since the money and reference was gone. There was a chance Mrs. Travers would ignore any inquiry. In her past dealings with the woman, she had acted reasonably—excluding the method of dismissal. Hopefully, the housekeeper would be fair.

"I'm grateful for your kindness and should not be taking out my disappointment over my current situation on you." Eliza nibbled absently on a piece of cheese. "I do apologize."

Stealing a glance at the man before her, she had to admit he *was* handsome in a formal, serious way. Besides the perfect cheekbones, he possessed a wide, sensual mouth, though it often pulled in a taut line of what she supposed could be complete disapproval.

"I'll travel to the village tomorrow if the roads are clear and see what employment I can acquire for you," he said. "It may be beneath your previous station as a governess."

No acknowledgment of her sincere apology. Well.

"I will do any honest work that pays a fair wage." Without thinking, Eliza gratefully clutched his hand, and he stiffened. His large hand was comforting. Unexpected warmth traveled through her, heating her blood.

Mr. Colson's silver-gray eyes widened, then he pulled his hand away from hers as if he had thrust it into flame. Stumbling to his feet, he clasped his cane and hobbled from the room, slamming the door behind him.

Not even touching the golden son of the earl caused such a powerful reaction in her as the mysterious, gloomy Mr. Colson had.

How unnerving.

Chapter 4

MISS WINSTON—ELIZA—COULD not stay here. Twice now, he'd fled her presence. In the past, Tremain never ran from women. In fact, many had sought him out. Indulging in sensual pleasures was once one of his favorite pastimes.

But that was long ago. Another life. Another man.

His oldest brother, Harrison, was more of a rake than any of them, or so his reputation stated, while Spencer lived the life of a studious monk. At one time, in years past, Tremain played it down the middle, much like his status in life. Though lately, he lived more like his younger brother than the oldest.

Tremain did not want an attractive woman under his roof. She upset his equilibrium and his plan to live a sober, solitary, and celibate life for the time being. Her touch had boiled his blood and hardened his shaft to the point of pain.

If he had his way, he would send her on to Dover and forget that she ever existed. Move on with his sedate life. He would head to the village in the morning and find her other accommodations even if he had to crawl through the snow to accomplish it, as she could *not* stay another night under his roof. The temptation to kiss her senseless, caress every inch of her luminescent skin was becoming harder to deny. His unexpected reaction proved he had gone too long without the intimate company of a woman.

Remove the temptation. Do my good deed, and move on.

Yes, it was a sound and sensible plan.

ELIZA AWOKE TO THE sounds of doors slamming. Stretching, she winced, her muscles protesting any movement.

Time to rise.

Bad enough, she'd used a chamber pot last night. How mortifying to have Mr. Colson empty it for her.

She sat upright. Pushing herself up with one hand, she stood. Though her legs shook, Eliza managed to walk back and forth without stumbling. Not too much damage, then. Grabbing the draperies, she pulled them back to reveal the sun shining high in the sky; the rays glistened on the blanket of snow, causing it to twinkle and shimmer. The storm had passed.

Now to locate her rescuer.

After dressing, she pinned her hair in a haphazard bun, opened the bedroom door, and peered out into the hall. Mr. Colson's house was a good size for a man living alone. She assumed he was alone, as no one else checked on her, nor had he mentioned other occupants or a family. But then, he didn't say much of anything of consequence in their brief conversations.

Eliza took note there were more rooms at the end of the hall. Tentatively, she made her way to the front of the residence. There was a parlor with a few pieces of high-quality furniture. About to head back through the hallway, the front door banged open, causing her to jump. The man certainly made an entrance. He was dressed all in black, from his boots, trousers, and long frock coat, all except for the stiff white collar—

Collar?

Eliza clasped her throat in shock. "You're a priest?" she rasped.

He bowed stiffly. "Reverend Tremain Colson at your service."

He is a vicar—not a Catholic priest, though that was bad enough. Humiliation covered her as she realized she had told her sordid story to a man of the church. No wonder he'd acted with cold disdain and wanted her gone from his sight.

"Why didn't you tell me?" Eliza motioned to her throat, pointing at her collar, her hand trembling.

"That I'm a vicar? Would it have made a difference?" One thick, black brow arched in question.

"Yes! I wouldn't have told—never mind." Eliza flushed, embarrassed to her core.

"You should return to bed and rest. The roads are not clear enough to head to the village. My trip will have to wait until tomorrow."

His voice was commanding and would brook no argument. Eliza was far too weary to mount a dispute over much of anything. Resing in bed sounded marvelous.

The vicar moved to her side and clutched her elbow. "Allow me to assist you."

Heat emanated from his touch, and instinctively she leaned against him. Besides the warmth, she reveled in the solidness of him. Shame on her for finding an Anglican priest attractive. She glanced at him as they slowly made their way to his room. He was a ruggedly masculine, cold marble sculpture.

Once in his room, he released her elbow. "I'll bring you a bowl of oatmeal and a cup of tea. You must eat."

Eliza didn't care for oatmeal, it reminded her of the industrial home, but he was right; she should at least attempt to eat.

"Yes. Thank you."

Mr. Colson turned and left the room, ignoring her gratitude.

Eliza quickly removed some of her clothes, leaving the chemise and blouse on her. As she crawled under the covers, the warmth of the blankets caused her to moan softly. Truthfully, she could use another day to recover.

It was providence that the snow hampered her departure. And where would she go? A lump formed in her throat. After everything that had happened, it would be easy to indulge in self-pity and have a cleansing cry. It wasn't in her nature anyway, and she was too exhausted to muster up a few tears.

Mr. Colson returned with a tray, laid it on her lap, and left the room without saying a word, closing the door behind him. She glanced into the bowl at the paste-like lump of oatmeal. At least he brought sugar. Eliza shuddered in distaste.

Scooping up a heaping teaspoon, she sprinkled it over the oatmeal. Hungry, she ate all of it and drank the tea; both warmed her insides. With a yawn, she laid the tray on the floor, curled under the covers, and fell fast asleep.

BY THE TIME ELIZA OPENED her eyes, darkness had filled the room. Once again, she'd slept the afternoon away. The sudden urge to urinate caused her to sit upright. Should she locate a water closet or use the chamber pot once again? In her brief exploration, the vicarage appeared modern enough. Indeed, he must have an indoor necessary, or even an outdoor one would suffice. She stood, then stepped into her wool skirt.

After doing up the buttons, she opened the door and peered out into the darkened hallway. Had Mr. Colson already retired for the night? Eliza made her way to the end of the hall. Splashing water halted her steps. Since the door was partway open, she glanced in. Mr. Colson stood with his back to her, having a sponge bath. He wasn't wearing a shirt.

What is the proper thing to do? Retreat unnoticed and return to her room. However, Eliza could not get her legs to move, for the sight of his broad shoulders and muscular back held her in thrall.

Her mouth went dry as he lifted his arm and washed underneath, muscle and sinew rippling under his skin with each movement. Eliza's concentrated gaze followed the cloth trail from under his arm to across his stomach. His shoulders and back tapered down to a slim waist. The tight trousers hugged a firm backside, and Eliza bit her lip, stemming an inappropriate moan of desire.

Mr. Colson turned to face her. Their gazes locked and held. Though mortified at being discovered, Eliza still could not find it within herself to flee. He lowered his arms, and she drank in the vision before her. Although he mainly stood in shadow, there was no mistaking that the front of him was as muscular as the back. Her gaze lingered; curly black hair covered his impressive chest. Her heated gaze slid to his face; she could have sworn she saw fire dancing in his eyes. Eliza's breathing came in short gasps. Did his nostrils just flare, or was it merely her overactive imagination?

Several moments passed.

The air between them cracked with life, with heightened and heated emotions Eliza could not even name. The spell broke when Mr. Colson turned and continued with his task. Taking a cleansing breath, Eliza backed out of the doorway, then fled for the safety of her room.

After a night dreaming of a particular muscular vicar, Eliza awoke feeling far from rested, for tossing and turning didn't translate into a soothing slumber. Her sexual experience was brief. The assignations with William Winters transpired quickly and under secret circumstances. During the two meetings, they had hardly removed any clothing.

But in her dreams, her fevered imagination had conjured a few sensual scenarios with Tremain Colson. The virility fairly oozed from the man. Perhaps she should feel ashamed of her feelings, but she didn't. They were perfectly natural; why deny it? Though she would keep them to herself and not act on them. Not *this* time. Lesson well learned.

Enough dreaming. Time to get on with the day.

Once dressed, she gathered her courage to locate the vicar, hoping he would not bring up the fact she'd found him half-naked and openly ogled him. Hunger urged her onward as she'd slept through supper and felt too mortified to venture out of her bedroom afterward.

Eliza located the vicar in the parlor. He stood, leaning on his cane, his face as brittle and cold as a sheet of ice, so much for their heated gazes of the previous night. Perhaps she'd imagined the entire thing.

"The road is passable enough to make my way to the village." Reaching for his long frock overcoat, he struggled to slip it on, and without thinking, Eliza stepped forward to assist him by lifting the coat up and over his shoulders.

The vicar pulled on his leather gloves as he spoke. "I'll make inquiries regarding accommodations and work. You cannot stay here another night."

No. I cannot tarry here. Not at all.

And not only because of her attraction to him. Eliza had no desire to share housing with anyone associated with *any* church, regardless of the denomination. Growing up in a Catholic orphanage consisted of duty, prayer, and cold indifference. Some of the nuns were kind, and she'd gained an excellent education and ultimately a good position, but there was no love or affection in her life. None at all.

That is why she eagerly and greedily took what William Winters offered. She could admit it now. Love, even the carnal, was a form of warmth. Intimacy. All the things Eliza lacked in her experience. All the things she yearned for. So much so she had abandoned all reason.

This tall, solemn man of the cloth had nothing to offer her despite his handsome face and form.

Eliza nodded briskly. "Yes, I cannot stay here."

His brow arched at her formal tone. "Very well, help yourself to tea and porridge in the kitchen." He clasped his cane and hobbled out the door, closing it behind him.

Eliza rushed to the window. It was then she saw the church to the right of the residence. In studying the weathered granite stone walls, Eliza concluded that the fair-sized structure was possibly a hundred years old or more. A wood spire topped the church with a large bronze bell within.

Mr. Colson climbed aboard a small gig, his movements awkward and stiff. Considering his damaged leg, she doubted he could ride a horse. With a snap of the reins, he departed.

Eliza watched until his broad-shouldered form disappeared from view.

How surprising that he left her alone. If she were so inclined, she could rob him blind, though there wasn't much of value. After inspecting each room, she located the one Mr. Colson had washed in and was amazed to find a tub and wash basin attached to pipes in the wall. Strange for a village vicarage. And an earthenware water closet. She used it, then cleaned the chamber pot before exploring further.

The two rooms at the end of the hall consisted of a guest room, where she assumed the vicar slept the past two nights, and a small study where he no doubt wrote his uncompromising sermons. As tempted to explore and discover more about the man, she backed out of the room and closed the door. Invading his private space seemed wrong.

The house was clean and neat, with sparse furnishings and non-existent personal touches as if he were a guest in his own residence.

Finding the kitchen, she gasped in astonishment at the bright, huge space. Two large windows in the far-right corner of the room gave the area a blast of sun, providing ample light and heat. A sizeable cast-iron cooker stood against the opposite wall, with various sizes of copper pans hanging above it.

But what truly surprised her was the oak icebox. The Bowater Manor owned one, but a vicar? Did he live under the auspices of a wealthy patron of the church? Grasping the heavy kettle, she turned on the tap and filled it halfway. Again, water in from pipes.

With the stove lit and the kettle on the burner, Eliza inspected further. The room was spotless. The pantry contained shelves full of all the staples required for preparing meals, and when she located a biscuit jar, she greedily snatched a few and ate them. Cold porridge sat in a bowl on the counter. As a governess, she could only claim a few cooking skills, such as a few nursery dishes, a cup of tea, and nothing else. In her previous position, servants brought her tray to the nursery.

Exhaling a wistful sigh, Eliza knew that those days of privilege— such as they were— were now at an end. Perhaps since she ate alone and maintained little interaction with the staff, it could be the reason she had never made any friends at the Bowater Manor.

The loneliness had been unbearable—trapped between two worlds—the servants and the served. Another reason she'd jumped at William's invitation. Deep in the dark recesses of her soul, she knew that the assignation was wrong and a terrible risk considering her position.

How reckless. Eliza had never acted in such a way that was so unlike her.

Or maybe it wasn't unlike her at all.

A loud hiss of steam pulled her from her ruminations of the past. Dashing a lone tear from her cheek, she vowed to stop reflecting on her mistakes—time to move forward and take what comes with courage and determination. Reaching for a cup and saucer from the shelf, Eliza nodded. *Yes.* Enough wallowing. Considering recent events, it would be an easy step toward a bitter, dark place and stay there—pondering over her fate.

Speaking of, what happened in the handsome vicar's past to have him hide behind a curtain of chilly indifference?

Chapter 5

THE TRIP TO HAWKSGREEN took longer than Tremain anticipated, but the sun had melted the snow enough that he could plow a path toward the village. During the journey, he could not tear his thoughts from Eliza standing in his parlor with her bruised and swollen face. She looked quite alone, at a loss and uncertain. He understood it and sympathized with it.

But the memory that seared his brain was her finding him washing last night. The air between them had sizzled with life. A good thing her gaze never lingered below his waist, for he'd been as hard as oak. It took all of his restraint not to cross the floor and pull her into his embrace. Kiss her senseless. Instead, he retreated behind the ice wall that he'd constructed for himself.

Although, he hadn't always been quite so cold and remote. When had the change taken place?

Tremain knew *precisely* when.

It was almost three years to the day at the Battle of Rorke's Drift in South Africa. Even thinking of the Anglo-Zulu war caused a blast of white-hot pain to shoot up his leg and settle in his upper thigh, tearing at his damaged muscles and cartilage with insistent claws.

No, not today.

Tremain banished the horrid memories from his mind as he pulled on the reins. The horse stopped before The Rusty Cockerel, the village's only inn, and pub.

The proprietor, Jonas Tompkins, a squat, jolly man, hurried out the front entrance to greet him, wiping his large hands on his apron.

"Well, now, Vicar. I didn't expect you in the village so soon after the storm. Unless poor Ruth Payne has taken a turn for the worse." Tompkins snapped his fingers toward the young lad standing nearby and instructed him to care for the horse and gig.

"That is my next stop." Tremain followed Jonas through the front entrance. Thick pipe smoke hung heavy in the air. Boisterous laughter filled his hearing, and the odors of beer and baking meat pies filled his nostrils. How tempting. Removing his hat and gloves, he passed them to Jonas, who set them on a shelf. "Could I have a quick word with you and your good wife?"

Jonas showed Tremain into his small office, then hurried away to fetch his spouse. The innkeeper returned with his wife, and they closed the door behind them.

"Good day, Vicar. What can we do for you?" Mrs. Tompkins smiled warmly. Her bright, friendly personality made her the ideal hostess.

The couple never acted discomfited by Tremain's abrupt manner and treated him kindly regardless of his ever-changing moods. Because of it, he allowed the granite mask to slip when alone with them, showing as much warmth and benevolence as he could muster.

"I'm hoping you might have a position and a small room for a young lady. I found her two nights ago at the height of the storm. She'd been beaten, robbed, and thrown from a carriage."

Mrs. Tompkins gasped, raising her flour-covered hand to her mouth. "Good heavens. How terrible. Jonas and I were discussing needing an extra hand in the pub. There be a wee room in the attic she could use, consider it part of the employment."

"Excellent. Miss Eliza Winston was previously a governess."

The couple exchanged dubious looks. "Well, Mr. Colson. Pulling pints in a pub is a lower position than a governess," Jonas said.

"To some, but considering her dire situation, I don't think Miss Winston would dismiss a chance at an honest job." Or so he assumed.

Wincing in pain, Tremain leaned on his cane to alleviate the agony caused by sitting too long. "Now that she's recovered from her attack and the storm has passed, she cannot stay in the vicarage another night."

Mrs. Tompkins nodded in agreement. "I see your difficulty. Bring the lass here later this afternoon. We'll get her settled. We'll pay nine shillings and sixpence a week to start."

"More than generous. I'll confirm Miss Winston's employment. When the lad is done seeing to my horse, I'd like him to run to Cranbrook to send a telegraph for me. The fact that Miss Winston stayed at my place the past two nights: let's keep it between us three, shall we?"

Jonas gave a brisk nod. "Aye, no one's business. Take a load off, Vicar. Sit in my chair a while."

With a sigh of relief, Tremain lowered himself slowly into the oak desk chair. Carrying in the voluptuous Miss Winston, then dragging in her large, heavy trunk, had taken its toll.

"Stay for lunch, Mr. Colson. Meat and potato pie with fresh cottage loaves hot from the oven. On the house for you." Mrs. Tompkins smiled.

"Charitable as always. I'll take you up on the invitation after I return from visiting with Ruth Payne."

"A pint of bitter as well?" Jonas winked.

"Yes, thank you. *That* I will pay for."

Jonas touched his forelock and followed his wife from the room. Tremain groaned in agony and massaged his numb leg until the tingling abated. At least he would be able to eliminate the temptation of Eliza from his immediate proximity. He wasn't sure how she would react about working at a pub, however temporary or permanent. Though she stated she was willing to do honest work.

Yes, the sooner Eliza was gone, the better.

Tremain held up the hand she'd clasped this morning. It still burned. The light scent of jasmine clung to his skin. Raising it to his nose, he inhaled deeply. Yes, still there—to tease and tempt.

There was no denying it. Tremain wanted her. He was thinking of her constantly—and thinking of her by her first name—all the more reason to push her away.

AFTER RELAXING IN JONAS'S office for more than a half hour, Tremain limped to the edge of the village where the fatally ill Mrs. Ruth Payne resided. Gossip traveled fast in Hawksgreen, more rapidly than a brush fire, and many of the residents doubted the ailing woman was ever married, but they allowed the tale to stand for the sake of her young son, Andrew, who preferred to be called Drew.

Ruth and Drew lived in a ramshackle bottom flat on one of the more run-down village streets. Since becoming seriously ill, Ruth couldn't keep her job as a laundress and had to rely on the good graces of her neighbors for food, rent, and the care of her nine-year-old son. Ruth lingered as the cancer inside her spread slowly and violently, attacking her internal organs individually. Doctor Edwards, who tended to patients in both Cranbrook and Hawksgreen, declared that she neared the end, merely a matter of days.

Upon entering the small flat, the smell of sickness and death assaulted his nostrils. Tremain would never get used to this part of his job. It reminded him too much of his time in the army: the battlefields and the sick and dying soldiers who lay upon them.

Drew Payne greeted him, his worried blue eyes staring up at him, unblinking and beseeching as if Tremain held the power to save his mum, which he did not. All he could do was offer hollow platitudes of sympathy and compassion. Yet, the young lad's heartbreaking misery thawed his heart a little.

Tremain briefly cupped Drew's flushed cheek, giving him a fleeting but empathetic smile. "Good afternoon, Drew."

The boy's lower lip trembled. "She's not good, Vicar. And we be running out of wood and food."

Tremain removed his hat and gloves and placed them on a rickety three-legged table. No wood explained the blasted cold. Under the circumstances, he would keep his coat on. "Take me to your mother, Drew."

Drew grasped his hand and pulled him along to the sick room. Inside, Ruth lay in her bed, her breath ragged.

Nearby, her neighbor, Mrs. McKinley, sat knitting. The older woman stood. "Thank God you be here, Mr. Colson. If you hadn't come today, I would've sent word. Things be dire."

"Drew filled me in. Mrs. McKinley, thank you for your continued kindness toward Ruth and her son. Send your husband along in about thirty minutes. I will pay him to fetch food and firewood."

His tone sounded commanding to his own ears, but someone had to take charge of this dismal situation. Mrs. McKinley clearly received the message as she quickly gathered up her knitting and, with a shaky nod, hurried from the flat.

"Drew, be a good lad and allow me to speak to your mother alone?" he asked softly. Drew nodded, closing the door behind him. Tremain pulled up a wobbly chair and sat by Ruth's bedside. Taking her thin, cold hand, he squeezed it gently. Offering comfort didn't come easily, but his compassion for this good woman was genuine.

"Won't be long, Vicar," she whispered hoarsely.

"No, Ruth. Not long at all."

"Promise me; you'll see Drew goes to a loving home?" Ruth coughed. "Though the neighbors have been kind, none of them want the boy, and-and I don't want him to wind up at one of those awful places. A workhouse or orphanage. Promise me?" She weakly clutched at his hand.

"I've already spoken to Viscount Hawkestone's steward, Mr. Jonathan Dibley and the wheels are in motion to find Drew a loving home. Lay your worries to rest. I give you my word. I will care for the child and see him settled."

A great sob left her throat. "Both you and his lordship have been a blessing. I've no family. What would've happened to us?" A bout of severe coughing interrupted her words. Blood trickled from the corner of Ruth's mouth.

Tremain reached into his pocket, pulled out a handkerchief, and dabbed the blood away with great care. "Though the viscount is an absent landlord, he's well aware of what goes on with all his tenants and the villagers. He's instructed me to see to your comfort. And to that of your son."

He laid his hand on her forehead. "Eternal God, grant your servant, Ruth Payne, your peace beyond understanding. Give us faith and the comfort of your presence." Ruth closed her eyes, tears escaping the corners and trickling down her cheeks. "I go and prepare a place for you. And I will come again and will take you to myself. Let's deliver the Lord's Prayer. Our Father..."

They recited the words together. Ruth's voice shook, but the benevolent smile she gave him told him he had given her a modicum of peace. At times like this—and they were rare—Tremain believed he did some good in the world.

Ruth closed her eyes and napped fitfully. Last week, Ruth had revealed the circumstances of Drew's birth, and Tremain promised to keep the secret and never show the tragic details to the lad.

Mr. McKinley arrived, and Tremain passed him the coin, barking orders to fetch food and firewood. He shouldn't be so stern; the neighbors did what they could as they had their own lives to lead and mouths to feed. But seeing a good woman suffer needlessly turned his bile. Tremain would ensure Ruth Payne's final days were calm, peaceful, and worry-free. When he departed, he would send word to Mr. Dibley to hire someone to stay with Ruth and Drew until the end, tending to their needs as he would tend to their souls. The viscount had promised assistance in this matter.

Then he would fulfill his promise and find a home for the boy.

Chapter 6

HOW LONG WILL THE VICAR be?

Eliza still could not believe her frosty but handsome rescuer was a man of the church. How could such an emotionally detached man offer prayer and sympathy to the masses?

Since she probably would never understand the machinations and inner thoughts of the vicar, she kept herself busy by unpacking her trunk. Moisture had seeped in, but thankfully, not enough to ruin her clothes or meager possessions. Eliza dried her clothes and the quilt by the fire, then changed into a new blouse and repacked everything. She had also managed to wash herself, although she gasped in horror at her bruised face and body. Mr. Colson had efficiently tended to her cuts and injured nose.

The incident with those two horrid men could have had a different outcome. Though it may be difficult, Eliza promised herself not to dwell on the fact that those horrible men nearly violated her.

Once she made her way to the kitchen, she heated a bowl of stew, sat in the parlor, and waited. She then waited some more, trying not to reflect on what had occurred in the past thirty-six hours.

Finally, a jingle of horses' harnesses caught her attention. Eliza ran to the window, and her gaze followed Mr. Colson to the small barn. Ten minutes later, he walked through the front entrance, the sun shining on his black hair. It was so dark; the shade appeared almost blue.

Leaning on his cane, he held his hat tightly in his gloved hand. "Good afternoon, Miss Winston."

She nodded and smoothed her skirt. "Good afternoon, Mr. Colson. Would you care for a cup of tea?" She acted as if she were the mistress of the house and he the visitor. It was the polite thing to do, as he'd been traveling out-of-doors and would be chilled.

"I thank you, no. Sit." Eliza gave him a skeptical look at his command. "If you please," he added. Sitting opposite her, he leaned forward, both hands resting on his cane. "I found you employment and a place to stay."

My, that was quick. Grass didn't grow under this man.

"I'm deeply grateful." And she was. The vicar was under no obligation to assist her, yet he had, despite his outward chilliness.

"It's good, honest work for good, honest people. It will suffice until you decide what to do next. The Tompkinses need assistance in their pub and inn and graciously offered you a position. They have a small room upstairs you can stay in, free of charge. The salary is nine and six a week."

In a pub? A barmaid?

Pulling pints while flouncing about in a low-cut peasant blouse while fat, sweaty men pinched her rear? She struggled to hide her disappointment. Perhaps the vicar thought this all she was suitable for considering her past—a foolish confession made in a moment of weakness.

"I know it's not ideal for someone with a governess background," he continued, "but I did say there is not much in the way of jobs in the village. I could take you to Cranbrook, a town of some two thousand. It's four miles away. There would be more positions to choose from."

"No. I'll accept the situation at the pub, and thank you."

Mr. Colson pulled out a slip of paper from his coat pocket. "I sent a telegraph to the housekeeper in Yorkshire. She replied swiftly and confirmed your employment. It's good enough for The Tompkinses.

They're kind, generous people, and discreet. They will not tell anyone you spent two nights here, nor should you."

Ah. Of course.

The priest must protect his reputation, and she couldn't blame him. Still, for some strange reason, it hurt that he wanted her out of sight and mind as soon as possible.

They stood. "I understand. You must protect your status within the church and village." Eliza nodded. "What type of woman travels in the dead of night, especially without a chaperone? One that is beaten and robbed? A woman that is not fit company for one such as yourself. Yes, I understand." Her voice did not conceal her annoyance.

Blast this man. Why he stirred her emotions—she could not say.

The vicar walked toward her, stopping at a distance of mere inches. She caught a scent of the outdoors: fresh air and pine. He leaned in; his warm breath feathered her cheek. "No, Eliza. I don't want you here because you are temptation personified."

Clasping a loose tendril of her hair, he wrapped it around his gloved finger, then lifted it to his lips and kissed it. Eliza looked up at him, stunned. For once, his silver-gray eyes were alive with emotions she could not hazard to guess. But in a blink, the icy glare returned. He released her hair and stepped back, creating a chasm between them wider than the actual distance.

What to say? Acknowledge the attraction that pulsed between them with a life of its own?

He was a man. Eliza noticed that salient fact the moment she'd clapped eyes on him. She needed a swift kick to find this man attractive directly after her scandalous dalliance.

No shame.

Best to let these moments of weakness—on both their parts—pass without comment.

"Then I best fetch my coat and hat so we can be on our way."

The left corner of his lips quirked, then settled into a taut line of indifference. "I'll need assistance with your trunk. Can you manage?"

"Yes, I can," she replied.

"Very well. I'll bring the wagon to the door." He exited with a swish of his long coat and a thump of his cane.

The sooner she was gone from here, the better. Regardless of the vicar's manner, this man enticed her.

And Eliza could not allow it.

TREMAIN MADE HIS WAY to the barn, muttering curses under his breath. What possessed him to let down his guard and admit that she rattled him? He didn't need a luscious young woman prodding his thin veneer of control. Grumbling, he entered the barn and hitched up the second horse, Tarsus, which would allow the previous one, Pegasus, to recover. The matched pair were getting up in years.

An entire day wasted seeing to this usurper of his well-ordered life.

Well, he had to travel to town today anyway. Complaining would not hasten the duty. It was a common Christian charity to assist someone. What angered him was not the young woman herself but the complicated emotions she had stirred in him.

By the time he led the horse and gig to the front entrance of the vicarage, Eliza had already dragged her trunk outside.

Once the trunk was situated, Tremain held his hand to assist her into the wagon. With a frown, she glanced at it, then at him, as if she loathed touching him.

Slipping her hand in his, a crackle of energy sparked between them. He could feel it even through their gloves. Sitting side-by-side provided no further relief from his aroused state. Try as they might to refrain from touching, the erratic movement of the wagon caused them to collide into each other from shoulder to lower legs.

"Are you feeling well, Miss Winston? Any ill effects from your unfortunate incident?" Tremain didn't want to have a conversation but sorely needed a distraction from her presence—and his unruly desire.

"Aching and bruised. But I will recover. Thank you for asking."

"I admire the way you've handled the situation. You take it in stride. Most young women would be quite hysterical by this point. Courageous of you." Now he paid her compliments as if he were a courting swain.

"Why, thank you, Mr. Colson. I feel you don't offer praise often, so I appreciate it." Sudden ruts made her lose her balance and fall against him again, causing another dip of his insides. Eliza slid back to her side of the bench seat. "When one is brought up in an orphanage, and a Catholic one at that, crying and feeling sorry for oneself is strictly forbidden."

"You're Catholic?"

"I'm nothing. I neither believe nor disbelieve in the existence of God. I don't subscribe to any religion. The term that applies to me is Agnostic. I recently read of the term in a magazine."

Tremain could not be more surprised. "Let me guess, *The Freethinker*?"

"How did you know?" she gasped.

"Read it myself." He snapped the reins, and Tarsus responded with a shake of his head and a faster trot. "Just because I'm a clergyman does not mean I no longer wish to know and understand what others believe. A free-thinking governess. Good for you, Miss Winston."

Eliza gave him such a warm, open smile that he nearly dropped the reins. "It's refreshing to find a man of the church open to other opinions. Good for *you*, Mr. Colson."

Her praise pleased him. Surprising since he was not a man who longed for adulation. They traveled along in companionable silence. The snorts from Tarsus were the only sound in the cool winter air.

"Are you from this area, Vicar? We're in the district of Kent, is that correct?"

He was unsure of what to reveal, if anything. Tremain usually kept his own counsel. "I was born near Hastings, in East Sussex. South of here."

"Really? I've never been. Regardless of the snow, it's a pretty bit of country. I think I'll like living in this area."

"You plan on settling here?" he asked. Having Eliza nearby would not assist his hope of avoiding the distraction she caused, as he had assumed her stay would be temporary. "What about traveling to Dover? I offered to pay."

"I appreciate the offer. But why not settle here? I've no family and nowhere to go. I prefer this village over Dover. I find cities too noisy, smelly, and boisterous. Do you agree?"

"I don't mind the city life."

"I've no desire to locate to Dover. Though living by the sea would appeal. I enjoy the sound of waves and the bracing salt air. Do you mind it? The sea, I mean."

This exchange was veering too close to intimate conversation. Best to keep his distance. His fault, and Tremain never should've started it. But he could end it. "What I do mind is aimless prattle on nonsensical subjects," he replied brusquely.

Eliza clasped her gloved hands in her lap and looked away. His rudeness silenced her for the rest of the journey. Tremain had accomplished what he wished: for her to leave him be.

It also managed to make him feel like a complete heel. Deservedly so.

INSUFFERABLE MAN.

For a brief period, they had a civilized chat. Tremain was obviously intelligent with opinions she would find pleasure in discussing. Beyond her annoyance, the vicar's dismissive tone *had* hurt her. She would not show it—though tears hovered at the surface.

They arrived at Hawksgreen. Two neat rows of buildings lined each side of the main road, either brick or Tudor style. Located at the opposite end of the village was a wooden windmill. With a pull on the reins, the vicar halted the wagon in front of the red brick building at the end of the street. The swinging wood sign above the door read 'The Rusty Cockerel.' A middle-aged couple burst from the entrance. The man snapped his fingers at a young lad standing nearby.

Mr. Colson slowly descended, then held out his hand to offer assistance. Eliza didn't want to take it, for her hand still tingled from the previous scorching touch. Blast the man for eliciting a physical response from her. But she could not refuse as the innkeeper and his wife looked on. It would be a grave insult.

Slipping her hand in his, he helped her down. Mr. Colson squeezed her hand slightly, causing her breath to catch. Heat traversed up her arm, and before she could react further, Eliza found herself in the ample embrace of Mrs. Tompkins. Eliza stiffened as she was not used to being held in such a way, especially by a stranger. Introductions were made.

"Oh, you poor, dear girl." Mrs. Tompkins clucked sympathetically. She stood back, keeping a firm grip on Eliza's arms. "Look at your lovely face. Don't worry, Vicar. We'll care for her."

"I do not doubt it, Mrs. Tompkins," he murmured.

"Tommy lad. Fetch the trunk and take it up to the attic room." Mrs. Tompkins gave Eliza a broad smile. "The room's been cleaned and aired out, and as soon as you settle in, we'll get a hot meal into you."

The woman's kindness was almost too much to bear. If Eliza replied, she would start to blubber.

"I bid you farewell, Miss Winston." The vicar—Tremain—gave her a stiff bow.

"Goodbye, and thank you."

She stood on the threshold and watched him depart. Eliza kept her gaze firmly on him until he disappeared around the bend.

It was then the tears came. Everything Eliza had been holding in. The exhaustion and the ramifications of her horrific experience.

But most of all, she lamented his departure.

For it left a gaping hole in her heart that made no sense at all.

Chapter 7

ELIZA SETTLED IN AS best she could. The older couple could not be more convivial. Instead of putting her to work immediately, they allowed her a couple of days to adjust to her new surroundings before the training commenced.

During that time, she learned how to operate the beer pumps and memorized the different varieties of beer and their cost. Since her staid governess wardrobe would not do, Mrs. Tompkins assisted her in selecting appropriate clothing for her new occupation. At least the peasant blouse had a high neckline, but Eliza balked at wearing the lace-up corset over it.

"I know it's not quite proper, my dear. But the customers do expect a certain look. You have a fine figure; why not show it off? More tips for you, and aye, more profit for us."

Eliza eventually agreed.

The dark green skirt and corset complimented the shade of her eyes and golden hair. Thankfully, the bruises on her face turned a light yellow and, in using a dab of powder, were not as noticeable.

Hours of operation for the pub ran from eleven in the morning until eleven in the evening. The pub was clean, neat, and welcoming, with dark panel walls. It wasn't overly large and consisted of long tables and benches, round tables and chairs, and two private booths near the corner fireplace. Though nervous about the first shift, it had been uneventful so far. The regulars seemed pleased, and the travelers passing through were polite enough. Though Eliza discovered as the customers consumed more ale, their voices became livelier.

Eliza hurried behind the bar and filled the tankards. Smoke from the men's pipes made her eyes water. She soldiered on, watching the door, hoping the tall, handsome vicar would pass through it.

Pathetic, but she couldn't shake Tremain from her mind. Why? What had he done to garner such secret adulation?

Well, except rescue her.

Could that be the reason she fixated on him? He certainly acted as a hero, albeit a grumpy and standoffish one. She also shouldn't be thinking of him by his first name. Eliza sighed as she gathered up empty steins and placed them on her tray.

If her ill-thought-out affair proved anything, it seemed she was more of a feather brain than she thought when it came to handsome men. Nevertheless, she'd seen more than one in the pub this day, and none of them caused a reaction from her—nary a ripple of interest.

Mrs. Tompkins brought out a tray of food consisting of meat pies, fresh bread, and mugs of steaming tea. The tantalizing scents tempted her. "Come and sit, Eliza. Time for a rest."

The pot man rushed behind the counter to change the kegs before returning to the kitchen to wash the glasses and crockery from lunch. The inn was eerily quiet.

"You're doing well, lass. Keep smiling, and the time will fly by," Mrs. Tompkins said. She buttered her bread and took a bite. "Turned out well, if I do say so myself."

Eating a morsel of the meat pie, Eliza moaned softly. She couldn't remember tasting anything quite so remarkable before. "Your meat pies are delicious, Mrs. Tompkins. No wonder it's busy here during luncheon."

"Thanks, my dear."

"I wonder if you can tell me anything about Mr. Colson."

Mrs. Tompkins's fork halted in mid-air, and she gave Eliza a knowing look. "Now that is changing the subject. Interests you, does he?"

Eliza could not stop the blush from spreading across her cheeks. She nodded.

Mrs. Tompkins chuckled, took a bite of the pie, then swallowed. "Cannot blame you a bit. The man is handsome enough and sends many a heart fluttering around here, including my own. I may be on the dark side of fifty, but I appreciate a fine, strapping man when I see one." She chuckled again, then sobered. "I don't know much. He be under Viscount Hawkestone's patronage, who brought him here a little over two years past. The vicar keeps to himself, living a quiet life, and though he be a stern sort of man, he has a heart well enough."

"Does he?" Eliza sipped her tea. She knew he had part of one or wouldn't have taken her in during the storm and seen to her recovery—and obtained her this job.

"He doesn't show it to just anyone. The vicar doesn't suffer fools lightly and lets you know it. As for his past life, I know nothing. Nothing at all."

"He told me he hails from the Hastings area."

Mrs. Tompkins's eyebrows shot up. "That be more than he told anyone around here."

So much for finding out about Tremain and his past.

"Is he closely acquainted with the viscount?" Eliza asked as she buttered a slice of the cottage loaf.

Mrs. Tompkins buttered another piece of bread and bit into it with gusto. "Who's to say? We've never seen hide nor hair of his lordship in these parts. Ever."

How strange. Usually, a member of the peerage made some sort of appearance at his country seat during the course of the year.

"His lordship be the second son of the Duke of Gransford. I hear he came into the title recently through his mother's side. Something to do with the queen bestowing it on him. I don't understand all those rules." Mrs. Tompkins continued between bites. "He's never been here. He sent his steward, Mr. Dibley, and hired a few servants, but other than that, he stays in London. Mr. Colson has weekly meetings with Mr. Dibley, and they handle the viscount's business. They also handle our concerns. Between the two of them, they serve this village." Mrs. Tompkins ran her bread through the gravy on her plate. "Some may say the vicar has a frozen heart, but he cares about us all and sees us well, I do no doubt that."

Eliza could hardly believe it. Such an austere man would barely possess anything as essential as warm feelings for his fellow man, though it must be required for his position as a priest of the Anglican faith.

How unfair of her to judge him so. The vicar *had* assisted her. She'd only see him lower his mask for a few moments, like when he'd caught her watching him as he washed, then again in his parlor when he admitted she tempted him. But even a man without a heart experienced carnal yearning. That must be it. She stirred his lust and nothing more. Tremain certainly stirred hers. Regardless, Eliza had the distinct feeling there was much more to the vicar than he showed publicly.

THE POUNDING WAS INSISTENT and incessant. A rhythmic beat grew ever louder, closer, like an approaching train hurling down the tracks. The effect was mysterious and frightening; Tremain could hear men's voices speaking of it fearfully. Tremain could see nothing, only hearing the thundering rhythm and then a haunting chant as accompaniment.

A war chant.

A Zulu war chant and march.

Four thousand Zulu warriors, battle-hardened and merciless, were about to overrun the small British garrison at the Rorke's Drift mission station. Sweating and lying on his bunk in the infirmary, Tremain could only wait out the battle. An injury to his upper thigh and an accompanying high fever hampered him from joining his fellow soldiers in the 24th Regiment of Foot. He drifted in and out of consciousness. Delirium made him weak, vulnerable— and utterly useless.

A private entered the room. "They're banging their spears against their shields! Thousands of them! They are going to kill us all!"

Tremain could hear snippets of the battle, the rifle shots, and screams. A few more ambulatory men fired shots from the windows, and the loopholes cut in the infirmary walls.

Flame engulfed the hospital. A Zulu warrior burst through the straw roof, dropping to the floor. The warrior repeatedly speared one of the screaming, sick soldiers helpless in his bed until he screamed no more. Tremain clutched the rifle he'd been given. Could he even use it? He thrust forward, hoping the bayonet would make contact with one of the warriors who now spread through the room like a plague of locusts.

He and his fellow soldiers were all going to die.

TREMAIN BOLTED UPRIGHT in bed, his breathing ragged and harsh. Cold, clammy gooseflesh rose around his neck and down his arms. Three years and he was *still* disturbed by these nightmares. As if reliving that terrible day wasn't enough, his thigh pained him to the point of madness. Be damned if he would take laudanum. He had enough of that during the first few months of his injury. Never would he wallow in such a drug-induced haze again—nor did alcohol help, though it took the edge off when the throbbing raged.

Unfortunately, his bottle of brandy was in a cupboard in his study. Could he even walk to the room to fetch it? Damn it all; he would crawl.

Swinging his leg around, he cried out in misery. He'd nearly lost the entire leg from the upper thigh down. A battlefield sawbones had wanted to hack it off. Tremain wondered now if it would have been better to let the quack take the damned limb and be done with it. Trailing his fingers across his naked skin, he felt the many raised scars and noticeable indentations. The Zulu warrior carved him like a piece of pork loin—his muscles and tendons destroyed.

"You will never walk again."

Well, he proved the blighters wrong, but at what cost?

Hanging onto the bedpost for dear life, Tremain pulled himself up, biting his lower lip until it bled. He stood absolutely still for several minutes until the agony lessened, then reached for his cane and hobbled slowly toward his study.

The sun hovered on the horizon casting golden shadows across the property. Tremain stood at his study window with a full tumbler of brandy clutched tight in his hand, watching the sunrise. Bad enough he dreamed of death, he would have to deal with it more directly today as the doctor did not expect Ruth Payne to see out the day.

Isn't this why he turned to the church after the army? He decided to give his life in service, hoping it would bring him some modicum of peace. To serve penance for the lives he'd taken in the name of Queen and Country.

Yet, he felt empty, unsurprising, as he'd left his heart and soul at that burned-out mission hospital in the Transvaal. He was a broken, wounded animal. Glancing at his desk, Tremain took notice of the unopened correspondence, specifically the letters from his parents and brothers. Also, in the pile lay a letter from a former lover, no doubt wishing to become reacquainted. The sickening scent of lilies emanated from the envelope, informing him the correspondence came from the widow, Lady Samantha Trimly, his mistress, before he'd departed for South Africa. He should toss it in the flames as he had her other letters.

Meaningless sex held no temptation for him. Not any longer. Especially not the debauched encounters he'd indulged in during his affair with Lady Trimly. With complete indifference, he hurled the letter into the fire.

Tremain sipped the brandy, the fire easing his thigh and leg ache.

Sex held no temptation? Liar.

Miss Eliza Winston tempted him.

Since the war, no woman had aroused him in such a stark way. The attraction was earthy but also hinted at something more profound, which disturbed him more than the actual desire itself.

With a decided grunt, he hobbled to his desk and sat.

No sleep was forthcoming. Tremain might as well attend to some of the mail. He should answer his mother's letter first. How his gregarious parents managed to spawn such eccentric sons was indeed puzzling.

Instead, his gaze drew to Spencer's letter. Wasn't he cloistered away at the hunting lodge in Wales, deep in research? How did he manage such a swift reply? Tremain thought it would be weeks before he heard from his brother. Curious, he opened the envelope and slipped on his reading glasses.

DEAR TREMAIN,

I arrived at Penhaven on January the eighth and did not come alone. I've met a woman I love and who loves me in return. Who would have thought it? I'll write again about Philomena, but for now, I wanted to address your concerns first.

You can continue your mission: you are the bravest man I know. You could have escaped either to Gransford Manor or to sunny climes. But you didn't. You've changed your life. You've changed. There is no going back or looking back. I've only just come to realize this myself.

I will be holding my head high. You can do it too, Brother. That is what you do next. Live. Heal. And we will all be waiting for you on the other side. Move forward. And come back to us.

Spence

THE ADVICE WAS SOUND. Tremain was well aware of what the answers were before he even posted the letter. But he needed to hear it from someone else. Spencer was the most logical of the three brothers and spoke the unvarnished truth. Tremain could remain here as vicar for a while yet. Continue with his work. Brave? No. Not at all. The complete opposite, in fact.

Spencer in love? Who was this Philomena?

She must be a remarkable woman indeed to be able to handle Spencer and all his foibles, strange ways, and moods. Of the brothers to find love first, he did not imagine it to be Spence. Nevertheless, he was delighted at the news. That was not a development he expected. His brother was happy. Tucking the letter in the envelope, he set it aside. Before he replied to it or any other notes, there was one he had to write.

After pulling a blank piece of paper from the drawer, he opened the ink bottle and dipped his pen. He would write to this housekeeper Mrs. Travers, in Yorkshire and request more detailed information on Miss Winston.

Eliza.

If the stubborn young woman was determined to stay in the village, he should be sure of her past since he'd recommended her to the Tompkinses. Admittedly, he wanted to know more for his reasons as well. The housekeeper should also be made aware of the robbery.

Continuing to sip his brandy as he scribbled away, he barely heard the knock at the front door. Frowning, Tremain glanced down at his naked state. He must stop traipsing about the house in the altogether. Gripping his cane tight, he made his way to the front entrance.

"Who is it?" he barked.

"'Tis Tommy from the inn. Mrs. Tompkins said to fetch you and get you to nip along sharpish if you be wantin' to catch the last breath of Ruth Payne and say your prayers and such over her."

Despite the terrible circumstances, Tremain smiled briefly. He doubted Mrs. Tompkins wanted the lad to use those exact words.

"Very well. I'll let you in in a moment, Tommy."

Tremain had watched helplessly as poor Ruth lingered in agony for months, wasting away before his eyes.

There was no mercy in life, but then he'd never seen any on the battlefield either. But he would try to bring her comfort and peace.

Too bad he couldn't muster any up for himself.

Chapter 8

ELIZA REPORTED TO WORK at three that afternoon, offering to help Mrs. Tompkins in the kitchen, slicing carrots and potatoes for the meat pies. It was all rather sobering. The governess position at the manor meant no manual labor to contend with. She never stopped to consider how hard others worked below stairs. How arrogant of her. How thoughtless.

Mr. Tompkins walked into the kitchen. "Where's Tommy? He should take food to Ruth Payne's. The vicar's there and has been since dawn. He and the boy, Drew, should eat."

"I'll take care of it; don't you worry none. Go on with your chores," Mrs. Tompkins replied. Her husband gave her a smile and an affectionate slap on her backside. Mrs. Tompkins flushed. "Go on, you wicked man. Be off."

The couple was loving and kind to each other and worked side by side as partners. It struck Eliza that she longed for such a devoted alliance, and if the relationship had a potent physical side, all the better.

"If you give me directions to the Payne home, I'll take the food," Eliza offered.

Mrs. Tompkins wiped her forehead with her sleeve, then held up her flour-covered hands as she worked with the pastries. "Bless you, my dear. If you could slap a few bacon butties together, I'd be thankful. There are slices of seed cake in the larder. You'll find a basket on the shelf."

Eliza gave the woman a warm smile as she made her way to the pantry. After assembling everything, she packed the food on brown paper, placed the items in the basket, then fetched her wool coat, gloves, and scarf.

The sun shone high in the clear blue sky, but a decided chill lingered. Thankfully, the village was small, and Mrs. Tompkins's directions were easy to follow. The farther she traveled, the more the structures became less prosperous. As she rounded the corner, she spotted a tall man and a small boy standing by the back entry.

No mistaking those shoulders.

Eliza ducked into a darkened alcove, out of their sight but not hers and near enough to hear the conversation.

"But why did she have to die, Vicar?" the lad sniffled.

Tremain laid a comforting hand on the boy's shoulder. "I've no words to explain why, Drew. I'll not say it is all God's plan because I'm not sure exactly what that means. Nor will I say your mother has gone to a better place. For how can death and finality be better than life and living?"

This is a priest?

Eliza was utterly fascinated by his words. No false platitudes or hollow clucks of sympathy. No droning on in prayer. He spoke the truth—his truth—to a child no less.

Tremain crouched down in front of Drew. "But know this. Her suffering is at an end. Your dear mother no longer has worries or responsibilities. She is truly at peace. Mourn her, miss her, and never forget her, lad. She loved you and thought only of you with her last breath. Remember her with love."

Drew sobbed and threw himself at Tremain, who looked shocked at the sudden embrace. His arms remained stiff at his side. A furrow appeared between his black brows. A few tears gathered on Eliza's lashes as she watched the anguish of not only Drew but also Tremain, unsure of how to react to the boy's desperate grasp.

Then Tremain hugged him, holding on for dear life.

"Yes, let it out, Drew. Let it all out." His voice was soft with emotion.

"W-w-what will become of me, Vicar?" Drew sniffled. "Nobody wants me." He gave Tremain such a distressing look of worry that Eliza's heart tightened.

"Tonight, you come home with me."

Drew wiped the tears from his face with the tattered sleeve of his coat. "I can?" he asked hopefully.

"Yes. Gather your things. Tomorrow, we'll discuss your future."

The boy gave him another hug, then disappeared through the entrance. Tremain stood, his shoulders slumped as he clasped his hands behind him. Slowly, Eliza backed out of the alcove and made her way to the front of the flat.

An older woman let her in, a neighbor, Eliza guessed. The woman pointed her toward the back alley. Clutching the basket close, she hurried down the narrow hall and stepped through the back entrance, closing the door behind her.

"Mr. Colson. Mrs. Tompkins sent along food for you and the boy," she said quietly.

He whirled around and faced her; all semblance of the warm emotion he'd shown Drew Payne was gone. Tremain stared at her with those uncompromising icy-silver eyes of his.

"I take it the poor woman passed," she ventured.

"About fifteen minutes ago," he answered, his voice as frosty as his glare.

"How sad for the boy. What will become of him?"

"There are plans in place. I've discussed it with the viscount in our various correspondences."

Eliza was not sure quite what to do or say. Give him the food and leave, she supposed. Smiling, she held out the basket to him. "Inside are bacon butties and slices of seed cake."

With an intense look, Tremain took a step toward her. He took another, then another, and Eliza moved in reverse until her back came in contact with the crumbling brick wall.

"Why you appeared here at this moment, I do wonder." His deep voice was gravelly, but he softly spoke the words. "With death all around me, you materialize to remind me there is life." Tremain stood close, the basket she held in front of her the only thing between them.

He leaned in; their lips were barely an inch apart. "Make me feel, Eliza. Prove to me that I do live. Kiss me."

TREMAIN DIDN'T CARE that he made such a forward request. For once, he didn't hide his emotions. After watching a good woman like Ruth Payne suffer for months on end, only to die in agony, Tremain selfishly wished to feel—something. Standing so near, he noticed Eliza possessed a smattering of tiny freckles across her bandaged nose. He inhaled a scent all her own, a mix of floral that reminded him of a spring garden of wildflowers. And jasmine.

Eliza moved closer, reached up, and rested her petal-soft lips against his. Despite the chill in the air, her lips were all warmth and fire. The sensation tore through him, heating his blood. The last of his tightly held restraints fell away, he cupped her face and dove in, and she opened and welcomed him. With a groan, he took the kiss deeper, desperation fueling him onward. How tempted he was to toss her little basket aside and press her against the wall so there would remain no doubt of his desire. For a blessed moment, he no longer felt pain in his wretched, mangled leg or his dark heart and soul.

The kiss grew fierce. Eliza moaned and returned it with equal enthusiasm. He wanted more.

He wanted to feel *everything*.

Through the haze of yearning, Tremain heard the door creak open. With haste, he released Eliza, snatching the basket from her arm.

Mrs. McKinley stood in the open doorway. "Vicar? Bob Taylor be here with the coffin."

"Yes. I'll be along directly." How amazing he could keep his voice steady, for inside bubbled a cauldron of emotions he'd not experienced in years. Perhaps ever. The door closed, and he was hopeful the neighbor had not witnessed their kiss. Since Eliza entered his life, he tempted condemnation and fate at every turn.

"Thank the Tompkinses for the food, and I thank *you*, Miss Winston, for bringing it." He gave her his best coldly polite tone, one he'd honed through his misery.

Eliza frowned, and flame crackled to life in her emerald eyes. "You're the most infuriating man I've ever met!"

"So I've been told at various times in my life." It was true. His brothers had told him more than once he could be maddeningly stubborn.

"You can't keep doing this. Pull me close, then push me away. I abhor such games," Eliza snapped.

"I assure you I'm not playing games. I also assure you this will never happen again."

Her laugh was brief and brittle. "Liar. It will. You *know* it will."

Eliza turned on her heel and marched out of the alley. Exhaling, Tremain reached for his cane which he'd left propped against the wall, and leaned on it for support. The pulsating stab of pain in his leg returned.

Eliza spoke the truth.

It *would* happen again, and he had no earthly idea how to avoid it.

CHAPTER 9

TREMAIN AND DREW ARRIVED at the vicarage at five in the evening, the sun nearly set. Since he'd known Ruth Payne's passing drew near, Tremain made all the arrangements beforehand. The funeral will take place tomorrow. There would be no viewing, no wake, as per her instructions. A small graveside service with a few mourners would see her laid to rest.

Unpacking the basket's contents, he bade Drew sit at the table as he passed him one of the bacon butties. The lad was quiet and had been since they left the village.

Tremain poured him a glass of milk from the pitcher. "It's cold and fresh. I have an icebox, if you can imagine. Eat up, lad."

Tremain sat, picked up his mug of hot tea, and took a sip. He watched the boy take small bites, his expression blank as if in shock. Death had a way of numbing those left behind.

"W-w-will I live here with you, Vicar?" Drew whispered.

"For a few days at least. Your mother's final wish was that you continue with your education." There was no school in Hawksgreen, but many of the children traveled to nearby Cranbrook thanks to the generosity of the viscount. Drew had not attended in many months, electing to stay home and care for his mother. Tremain could not fault the boy. It showed compassion and a sturdiness of character that spoke well of him. It was one of the reasons the viscount wanted the child cared for.

"You're going to send me away to school? Far away?" Drew's lower lip trembled.

"No. Don't worry. Not for a couple of years, at least. The viscount will hire someone to tutor you, so when you attend a boarding school, you will be at the same level as the other lads." Tremain gave Drew a brief smile. "I'll take you to the estate in a few days."

Drew's eyes grew wide. "I'm going to live with The Hawk?"

Tremain hid his smile of amusement at the viscount's nickname. "No, he's not in residence. But Mr. Dibley, his steward, lives there along with a few members of the staff. Also, there will be a governess for you. You'll learn the ways of a gentleman, among other things. Your mother died in peace knowing you would be given every opportunity at life."

Drew frowned. "But...why me?"

Why indeed? Drew would grow up to be a fine-looking lad with his clear blue eyes and tawny locks. He was intelligent and kind, and it was a damned bloody waste to let him founder in menial jobs such as working at the local grain mill. The truth of it? Drew was an experiment. Tremain wanted to give back to humanity; this deserving young boy was an excellent place to start.

"Because you're worthy of it, lad. Now, eat up. There's seed cake when you finish."

Drew nodded and bit into the sandwich.

A governess.

Eliza's arrival had proved to be prudent after all. The idea came to him last night. He'd wait a day or two, then offer her the position.

THE FUNERAL COMMENCED without a hitch, and the weather cooperated by providing another sunny, crisp day. When Tremain finished saying prayers over the grave, the few mourners headed to the vicarage for a repast provided by the Tompkinses. Eliza did not attend. She stayed behind to ensure the smooth running of The Rusty Cockerel. Tremain had spoken with the Tompkinses about his suggestion of Eliza becoming a governess, and they approved wholeheartedly, agreeing not to say anything until he could broach the subject to her.

Two days after the funeral, he and Drew headed to Hawkestone Estate. The church and vicarage were situated on the far southern tip of the property, and the house itself sat on a hill overlooking the valley and village of Hawksgreen.

The place consisted of forty rooms, not huge as manor houses go, but an adequate size for the country seat in which it sat. The brick residence was Georgian in style, with plenty of pillars, chimneys, and windows. The surrounding grounds bordering the estate were not ostentatious but simply kept. Of course, in January, all looked bleak. At least most of the snow had melted.

Only a barebones staff remained since the viscount was away from the residence. Besides Mr. Dibley, a footman acted as an under butler, a housekeeper, a cook, two maids, and a groundskeeper who also attended to the stables.

Treves, the young footman, greeted Tremain at the front door and showed them into the study. After several minutes Mr. Dibley entered. "Well, good to see you again, Vicar. And this must be the young lad we've heard so much about." Dibley turned to Drew and held out his hand. "Good to meet you, young sir."

Drew blinked, then glanced at Tremain questioningly, unsure what to do next.

"Take Mr. Dibley's hand and shake it, lad, and reply in kind," Tremain encouraged.

Drew did. "Good to meet you—sir."

Mr. Dibley smiled. "Well met. We have your room ready. Ah, and here is Anne to escort you. She'll be seeing to you until your governess arrives."

Drew shrank back, leaning against Tremain for comfort. All this must be overwhelming to the poor boy. "It's all right. Go with Anne. I'll see you before I leave. Remember, this is your home now. Be brave, lad. Remember your mother."

Drew looked at him, moisture swimming in his eyes. But he nodded, took Anne's hand, and exited the room.

"Well, my lord. Everything seems to be going according to plan."

"Jon, what have I told you?" Tremain hobbled across the room and closed the door. "Don't refer to me as 'my lord,' not even when we're alone. It may slip out when we're in the company of others."

"Of course." Dibley smiled. "Honestly, Hawk. How long are you going to continue with this charade? It's a wonder you haven't been found out. Also, I received a letter from your father, and he's greatly concerned you haven't answered any of your correspondence, particularly from your dear mother."

Tremain's eyes narrowed in annoyance. "Don't call me Hawk. And as to the letters, I've been busy. Besides, my family agreed to stay away and let me be. But I'll answer the letters, all of them."

"Good. Your father threatened to show up unannounced to see for himself that all was well. You know he will do it."

Yes, his father would do that. All is well was debatable, and he'd answer the letters as soon as possible. His father showing up would complicate matters. "To continue. Being a vicar is not a 'charade.' You were with me at Cambridge. I took all the requisite courses. I have my Masters in Divinity, and the archbishop ordained me."

"Steady on, Trey. I only meant that you could serve the tenants and villagers just as well, or even better, as Viscount Hawkestone instead of Reverend Colson."

Jon Dibley was his close friend. They'd known each other since they were lads. Jon's father still served the duke as a steward. When Tremain went to school, the duke generously offered to pay for Jon's education. Jon was offered the post of steward to Tremain's older brother,

Harrison, the heir to the dukedom, but their friendship and bonds were strong, and when the time came, Jon elected to serve Tremain instead. Jon was a true friend, and Tremain loved him as much as his brothers. Which meant he took Jon's advice to heart.

His leg groaned in protest at standing still too long, so Tremain sat on the sofa and exhaled in relief. Jon sat next to him.

"Serve just as well? Not in my mind," Tremain declared firmly. "People will tell a priest far more than someone from the peerage. Besides, this way, both the vicar and the viscount are working in tandem to ensure the health and happiness of everyone concerned. It's a sound plan. Even I think of the viscount as a separate entity in my thoughts, which is strange."

"And what of *your* health and happiness?" Jon asked, his voice soft with concern.

"It's not something I reflect upon."

"And how long will you play a dual role? As I said, how long before you pay your penance in full? It's sheer luck you haven't been discovered yet."

"To answer the first part of your question, I do not know how long. Until I find some modicum of peace, I suppose. Until I've paid back my debt."

"Good God, Trey. You owe no debt to society. You fought in a war. Like any soldier would do."

"The debt is owed; I feel it here." Tremain held his hand over his heart. "I'm aware this cannot continue; it's been two years already. As you say, it's a wonder the subterfuge hasn't been discovered as yet. Thankfully, my past acquaintances or paramours do not frequent this corner of Kent, so for now; I'm safe."

Jon frowned. "You're hiding away."

"Yes, damn it all, I am. I need—to heal. I'm a mess, Jon. Yet every time I help someone in my way, a part of my damaged soul is repaired. I don't know how else to make you understand. I barely understand it myself." Tremain laughed cynically. "I'm a sorry excuse for a priest. I'm not pious at all. It's why I initially went into the army instead of the church. I believed that my talents would be better served on a battlefield. How arrogant of me. And as for being a viscount? It's a bloody courtesy title. It holds no real meaning."

Jon shook his head. "Don't disdain it. You've had a great honor laid upon you, and the title is not a 'courtesy.'"

Viscount Hawkestone was an extinct title on his mother's side, going back more than one hundred years. Tremain hadn't asked for this accolade, but according to his father, the Queen wished to reward Tremain for his services to the crown by resurrecting the title through letters patent. One did not turn down Queen Victoria. He suspected the Queen wished to please the duke, as his father was a particular favorite at court.

"Regardless of what you think, the title holds meaning, Trey. It holds respect and responsibilities." Jon folded his arms. "Granted, you're wielding the designation of viscount in a meaningful way behind the scenes, but I firmly believe you could do far more if you stepped out from behind the curtain and embraced the power that comes with it by serving in the House of Lords. There you can effect *real* change. Ultimately, it's your decision. You know that I will support you."

"I don't like asking you to speak falsehoods, nor do I like asking it of my family. They're telling everyone in our social circle that I'm in Italy, basking in the Mediterranean sun to heal all that ails me. The ruse is holding for the time being. I ask for a little longer, Jon. Please have patience with me. I need to work this through."

"Very well. Patience."

"I appreciate it. And your friendship and support."

"So, we're to become a home for foundlings and indigents, then?" Jon's eyes twinkled in merriment.

Tremain nodded, giving Jon a brief and all too rare smile. "So it would seem, my friend."

Chapter 10

ELIZA WORKED DILIGENTLY at the pub for the remainder of the week and, while carrying out her duties, realized that the Tompkinses didn't need another barmaid. They'd hired her as a favor to the vicar. She thought about how long she could stay at this post constantly. Though she came to appreciate hard work and acquired new respect for those who labored long hours for little pay, she concluded that working as a barmaid for the rest of her days did not hold any appeal.

Being a governess is all that mattered. St. Anne's Industrial School had its faults, but she gained a solid education, finishing at or near the top of her class every year. The nuns stressed the importance of modest dress and deportment, an absolute must, and the ability to melt into the background. Her previous salary of twenty-five pounds a year had been more than generous for a governess.

Eliza was happy to find all the items in her trunk. Yet, in her two-year employment, she'd hardly saved a farthing. Growing up with nothing meant that having a few pounds in her pocket had made her giddy, hence buying books, the quilt, painting, and other little touches and trinkets to personalize her room.

Regardless, she imagined her whole life ahead of her, with plenty of time to save money and develop more frugal spending habits. Another lesson learned. After all, Susanna was only six. There were even discussions that she could become Susanna's chaperone and companion when the girl grew older. Eliza destroyed all those plans.

After growing up with a gaggle of rambunctious young girls and reveling in friendships, the nuns thrust her into a solitary life of quiet study and repetitive tedium. Losing track of her former friends hadn't helped. Many had found positions in far-flung corners of the country, and their duties meant no time for letter writing. Why had she placed her rosy future in jeopardy for a bit of warmth in the arms of a willing young man?

Alone and lonely.

Not an easy thing to admit under most circumstances, but in this case, all her hard-won common sense fled in the face of a handsome son of an earl.

But beyond all that, why, of all men, did she ache for—what did Mrs. Tompkins call him? 'The vicar with the frozen heart.'

Their potent attraction was hard to ignore, especially after that searing kiss in the alley. How dare Tremain lean in and whisper in her ear, kiss her with a fiery desire the Honorable Mr. Winters could only aspire to? If Eliza possessed any sense, she would gather her few earnings and relocate elsewhere. Forget she'd ever met the implacable Mr. Colson.

She should write to Mrs. Travers and obtain another copy of the reference, such as it was. At least she could apply for positions commiserate with her training. Registering with the Governesses Benevolent Institution would at least put her on a list for any available situations. Unfortunately, there were more governesses than available jobs. Until she received an answer one way or the other, she could continue working at the pub.

In light of her revelations and the new plan, she posted her letter to Mrs. Travers, explaining her situation with the robbery and attack and the loss of her money and reference. She did not ask for more monetary compensation; she would forgo it for a decent and honest appraisal of her work performance that would *not* mention the reason for dismissal.

Eliza was unsure how much the vicar relayed in his telegraph to the housekeeper. Still, she laid herself bare, apologizing again for her weakness of character and the shame she brought on the house, family, staff, and the position itself. Eliza did feel contrite and more than a little ashamed. In truth, she also wished to report those men for robbing her. Hopefully, the family will dispense some form of justice—time to admit past blunders and move onward.

Eliza no sooner stepped across the threshold of the inn when the young lad, Tommy, informed her that Mr. Colson awaited her in the office. Her heart thumped rapidly. Curse the man for having this effect on her. Hanging her coat and scarf on the hook outside the office, she smoothed her skirt and pulled the peasant blouse closer to her neck. Tremain had never seen her in her barmaid uniform. She knocked, then entered, closing the door behind her. He stood by the window, staring out into an empty alley.

"You wished to see me, Vicar?"

Tremain turned to face her. For a brief moment, the mask slid away as his gaze slowly took in what she wore from head to toe. He flushed an actual show of emotion and muttered, "My God," before shaking his head to dismiss her appearance and his reaction. He liked what he saw. A slow fissure of satisfaction moved through her. The calm facade was back in place when he looked her in the eye.

"Yes. I am here on behalf of—"

Eliza held up her hand to silence him. He didn't like the interruption, for the proof lay in his frown. "I have a question, and I'd appreciate an honest answer. Why did you kiss me in the alley last week?" she asked, her voice clear and steady.

Tremain muttered under his breath and turned away, facing the window again.

"And don't tell me it was merely to feel alive in the face of death, though I understand the purpose. There is more. Tell me." She stepped toward him, gently laying her hand on his wool coat sleeve. The muscles tightened under her touch.

"I suppose," Tremain replied gruffly, "It's the usual rationale when a man kisses a woman. I desire you."

Eliza closed her eyes briefly.

Yes. The truth at last.

"Regardless of my confession to you," she said softly. "I'm not a woman of loose morals. I made a mistake, a rather grave one that cost me my position and more besides. Believe me, I was under no illusions that the young earl's son cared for me, nor do I harbor deep feelings for him. I wanted —like you—to feel. Something. *Anything.* Warmth. Affection. I was lonely. Perhaps I still am." She clutched his arm a little tighter. "If you desire me, why are you so...unapproachable? So remote? Are you like this with everyone or just me?"

"You're not making this easy, are you, Miss Winston?"

"When we're alone, call me Eliza, as you did before. And no, Tremain, I'm well aware I am not making this easy. If I possessed a lick of common sense, I would ignore what passed between us and leave this village at the earliest convenience. I certainly wouldn't bring it up in conversation. I seem to be deficient in any sort of sense at all. Especially where you're concerned, answer me, please. Why are you so cold?"

He turned to face her. For once, the icy mask was not in place. Instead, he showed confusion and vulnerability.

"Perhaps you *should* leave. You disturb me, Eliza. You're shaking the very walls I placed around my heart. Cold? Remote? I suppose I am and have been since—"

"Since when?"

Tremain shook his head in dismissal. "It's of no matter."

"You've told me this much," she said softly. "Tell me what you were going to say."

He hesitated. "The war."

"What war? In Egypt?"

"No. The Anglo-Zulu War. I'm not here to discuss me. I desire you, but I will not act upon it."

She let her hand drop. The matter was closed. The war explained the injury to Tremain's leg and, no doubt, his disposition. Eliza had read of the returning soldiers' plights in the newspapers. Many had a difficult time adjusting to civilian life. Was Tremain one of them? Zulus? Wasn't there a horrible slaughter of British soldiers three years ago?

Tempting as it was to express doubt at his statement that he would not act upon his attraction toward her, Eliza never said that *she* wouldn't pursue it. However, caution would be prudent if she explored what lay between them. That is if she were even staying in the area.

"I apologize for being less than polite to you. I shall endeavor to act more of a gentleman in the future." The mask slipped back into place. Fine, she would let it go—for now.

"Thank you. I accept your apology. Why *are* you here?"

Tremain cleared his throat. "I'm here on behalf of Viscount Hawkestone. He's instructed me to offer you a position. As governess."

Eliza blinked rapidly in disbelief. Surely, she heard incorrectly. "A-a governess? Where?" she whispered.

"To the young lad, Drew Payne. He's in residence at Hawkestone Estate."

"He is? How?"

"His lordship agreed to see to the lad. Now, concerning the position. If you accept the situation, you'll be living there as well. With a generous salary and benefits. The viscount will match your previous salary and add bonuses to be discussed in the future."

What to say? It was the answer to her most sincere wishes and hopes. Honestly, she felt like crying, throwing herself at Tremain in relief. A lone tear trickled from the corner of her eye. She tried to look away, but Tremain spun her about to face him. They stood close enough that his alluring scent filled her senses. He laid his cane on the desk, pulled off his gloves, tossed them aside, and followed the wet trail down her cheek with the tip of his finger, leaving flame in its wake.

"Not all is dire. You've another chance at life." Tremain's voice was tender and comforting, making more tears escape. "Drew will need intense schooling as he has missed many months due to his mother's illness. He will need to learn deportment and the ways of a gentleman. The viscount has made Drew his special project, so you must prepare the lad to enter the echelons of higher education. Are you up for the task, Eliza?"

Blast the tears, her eyes were blurry, and a large lump had lodged in her throat, making speech nearly impossible. Instead of speaking, she nodded.

With a last swipe of his finger, he gently brushed away her remaining tears. "Good. Then that's settled."

Tremain turned and reached for his gloves and cane. By the time he faced her, all vestiges of tender concern were gone. The man was as annoyingly changeable as the January weather.

"The viscount will send his carriage in two days, at noon. The Tompkinses know the offer and will not stand in your way." He moved to leave.

"Tremain." Her voice trembled with emotion. "Thank you."

"Nonsense," he dismissed curtly. "I was merely delivering a message." He limped from the room, banging the door behind him.

Eliza knew he'd arranged all of this. Yes, the viscount had agreed, but she had no doubt the plan was all Tremain's. A rush of unknown emotions flooded her, clutching her heart tight.

No, she could not fall for this troubled, damaged man regardless of how much she was attracted to him.

Chapter 11

TREMAIN COULD NOT SAY what possessed him to accompany the carriage to fetch Eliza. Perhaps it was his duty to escort her to Hawkestone Estate and introduce her to the staff and Drew. Or maybe he ached to see her again.

For two restless nights, he tossed and turned, imagining Eliza lying flat on a table with her long, shapely legs spread while he licked and tasted her until she cried out in ecstasy. He had affairs through the years. Since South Africa, there'd been no one. It could explain why the luscious Miss Winston whipped him into a froth.

Undoubtedly, he'd acquired enough discipline to push her away. Denying his baser emotions (and vices) had worked thus far. Yet, here he sat. For he could admit, he *did* ache to see her. Touch her, however innocently. Speak to her. Be in her presence.

The most disturbing aspect? Tremain would see her more often, as he met with Jon once or twice a week, and also promised Drew he would check in regularly. Since the vicarage and church sat on the edge of the Hawkestone Estate, it was a "good stretch of the legs" to the main house.

Tremain walked for exercise, hoping it would elevate some of the pain from his leg and thigh. The injury had ensured that riding a horse was no longer viable. How he missed it. Unfair, yet why bemoan the fact? At least he still lived, though that could be argued.

Blast it. Tremain's mind was scurrying about in all directions. He should have thrust a roll of banknotes at her and sent her along by mail coach to Dover or Ashton days ago. There she could've caught the train to whatever destination she wished.

Far from him, his desires and static, lustful nature.

Not so dormant now.

Tremain was pulled from his ruminating thoughts when the carriage abruptly stopped in front of the inn. The young man Jon had just hired, Terrance Jackson, jumped down and opened the door, pulling down the metal steps to allow Tremain to exit without too much effort.

Eliza stood outside, demure in her wool coat buttoned primly to her chin. The bruises had faded, and the plaster was no longer on her nose. With the swelling gone, he found her even more attractive. The scarf wrapped around her head hid her glorious golden locks. The thought of running his hands through her stunning hair hardened him further. Thankfully his long greatcoat hid his inappropriate response.

"I didn't expect you, Vicar."

"I should do proper introductions to Drew and the staff."

She gave him a warm smile. "Thank you."

Their gazes locked as if held in place by an invisible bond. Similar to the night she walked in on him bathing. Heat covered him inflaming his desire once again. Never had a woman caused him to react so swiftly. The Tompkinses noisy entrance broke the spell.

"Get on the stick, lads, load the trunk," Mr. Tompkins bellowed to Tommy and Terrance. They snapped to action. Mrs. Tompkins looked back and forth between him and Eliza, her eyes narrowing shrewdly. Tremain grunted and turned away, willing his cold mask to slip into place.

"My dear Eliza," Mrs. Tompkins said, her tone warm and friendly. "Here's your wages and a little something extra. There are meat pies and currant cake in the basket. Share some with Drew. He's a good lad, and you'll both get on well, of that I've no doubt."

Mrs. Tompkins gave Eliza a hug and a pat on the back before she stepped away.

"I cannot thank you both enough. You treated me with kindness. I'll never forget it," Eliza said, her voice trembling.

"Don't be a stranger, lass. You're welcome anytime," Jonas Tompkins declared.

Tremain held out his hand, assisted her into the carriage, then climbed in after her and closed the door. With a snap of the reins, the carriage pulled away, and Eliza waved to the couple until they turned the corner. Sighing wistfully, she sat back, her gloved hands clutching the basket tightly.

"You'll miss them," Tremain said.

"I will. The Tompkinses welcomed me into their lives and treated me with a benevolence I did not expect. Or even deserve. But you knew they would be kind when you approached them, didn't you?"

"Of anyone in the village, I knew they would care for you. They're the most generous people I've ever known. After your attack, you needed gentle empathy and understanding, and the Tompkinses were the ones to give it."

"But not you," Eliza whispered.

"No. Not me. Besides, you couldn't have stayed at my residence."

"The Rusty Cockerel didn't need another barmaid," she smiled.

"No."

"I have to ask. Shouldn't Drew have a male tutor to prepare him for his future?"

Tremain sat forward, leaning on his cane with both hands. "I'm aware a boy of a certain age should have a male tutor, that it is the 'done thing.' But Drew's education has been sporadic at best. There's no village school. The children travel to nearby Cranbrook, and Drew missed much time due to his mother's illness. Besides the fact, the lad has suffered a devastating loss. I believe an intelligent woman would be a good influence on the boy. A nurturing one." He shrugged. "Something men, in general, lack."

"You have a fair point. Who pays to transport the children to Cranbrook?"

"The viscount pays a man to take them by wagon. It's only a few miles. He also pays the Cranbrook Grammar School to educate them."

Eliza smiled. "Let me guess; it was your project, to begin with."

Damn, the woman for seeing through him. "Bah. It was cheaper than hiring a teacher and housing and feeding her in Hawksgreen," he replied dismissively. "The viscount agreed."

"And yet, his lordship is sparing no expense for the education of one solitary boy."

Tremain grunted again. This conversation was dangerously close to revealing his true identity. "Drew is a special case."

"To you or the viscount?" she asked softly.

"What does it matter? You have a respectable position once again. I wouldn't advise acting ungrateful." What a grumpy bastard he'd become.

"In other words, keep quiet and do the job," Eliza bit out, obviously growing annoyed. He couldn't blame her.

"Sound advice. Take it." Tremain looked away, staring out the window. The snow had melted, making the roads slushy and slow to traverse. The overcast skies emitted a bleak illumination that pretty much matched his mood. It was a mistake to come. In trying to suppress his desire for her, he acted like a cranky, cold fish—more than usual.

"I don't mean to pry or probe," Eliza ventured. "I'm very grateful to you and the viscount. His lordship wouldn't have considered me for the position if you hadn't suggested it. Thank you." Her voice trembled at the last two words. Eliza took a deep breath and exhaled. "You hardly know me, yet you spoke for me. I owe you so much—"

"All I did was check into your former employment," Tremain interrupted. "I sent telegraphs and posted a letter, which I hope to receive a reply soon. You show an innate intelligence and a kindhearted nature that would benefit the boy. There's nothing left to be said."

Her gratitude irritated him further, making her all the more attractive and appealing. Eliza Winston was a glorious woman in all ways. Beyond her looks, that very intelligence and kindheartedness burrowed deep in his soul, shining a light where only darkness had resided these past years. Tremain also admired her forthrightness about her situation and did not hesitate to ask him direct questions, such as why he kissed her.

He wanted to kiss her now. Desperately. And that fueled his fury even more.

THE COLDLY SPOKEN WORDS took Eliza aback. It was as if two men resided in him. How to reach the compassionate one hidden away? Why not tell him she'd witnessed it firsthand? Be hanged if she would allow this obstinate man to put her off. Or make her angry.

"You care for Drew. I saw you in the alley with him shortly after his mother passed, and I overheard the conversation. I observed your face when he embraced you and how warmly you eventually responded. Do not act as if you're merely following the viscount's orders, for I've seen the proof. Your coldness is counterfeit."

A growing vehemence unfurled within him; she saw it reflected in his silver-gray eyes. It would not put her off.

"How dare you presume to know my innermost thoughts? You possess the unmitigated gall to eavesdrop on a private conversation? You've no earthly idea what I've endured, what I've witnessed—"

"Then tell me," she whispered.

"I'll never tell a living soul. Certainly not you."

Her heart contracted in pain at his unfeeling words and attempts to push her away. The stubborn vicar didn't know her well, for this declaration made her all the more determined to breach his icy wall.

"I came upon the two of you quite by accident. I admit to lingering longer than I should. But what you told Drew was frank, honest, and from your heart. You have one, don't deny it. Your flashes of temper don't frighten me. If we're to be friends, you'd better become used to me speaking my mind."

His eyes widened as if in disbelief. "You cannot be serious. Friends?"

"Why not? We both have a common goal and interest: Drew Payne." She shifted from sitting opposite to next to him. His large frame nearly occupied the entire space, and once again, she caught a whiff of his titillating cologne. She laid her gloved hand on his coat sleeve and gave it an affectionate squeeze. "You're a man whose friendship I would welcome. I don't want us to be hammers and tongs whenever we're in each other's company. Especially not in front of the boy. He's been through enough."

Eliza waited. Would he shake off her hand—and her offer of friendship? With a harsh harrumph, he clutched her gloved hand in his and held it, then turned to gaze out the window. They sat together for a while as the heat from his touch warmed her more than any heated brick at her feet could.

"Yes. For the boy," he murmured.

Oh, well done, Tremain.

Eliza smiled. Finally, she managed to slip past the first hurdle in her mission to reach his heart. The steep climb would be challenging, but this man was worth the effort to her.

Oh, so worth it.

Chapter 12

THE CARRIAGE PULLED up in front of Hawkestone Estate, and only then did Tremain release Eliza's hand. Her heartfelt offer of friendship nearly did him in. Even after his pointed and cutting claim of 'certainly not you.' He'd only meant that he wanted to protect her from his darkness, but it came out spiteful and harsh. Was he deserving of her kindness? Never. But he would take it nonetheless. Gratefully.

The carriage door opened, and he assisted Eliza in descending. His focus then turned to Drew. As Eliza wisely stated, the young lad needed them both, and subjecting Drew to a tense environment was not judicious for any of them.

Once shown into the main parlor, a maid assisted them with their coats, and as she departed, Jon Dibley entered the room.

"Mr. Dibley, may I introduce Miss Eliza Winston?" Tremain said.

Jon gave him a side glance with a raised eyebrow, and Tremain knew precisely what the expression meant, for he'd neglected to inform him that Eliza was young and attractive. When Tremain observed the warm smile Eliza gave his friend, a stab of jealousy slid beneath his ribs.

Should I be worried? Hell, where did that come from?

Jon held out his hand. "It is wonderful to meet you, Miss Winston. You will be a welcome addition to this house. I'm Jon Dibley, steward and land manager of the Hawkestone Estate."

"Thank you." She gave Jon another warm smile, which caused the stab of jealousy to slide further in, taking a twist for good measure.

"Master Andrew Payne, who prefers to be called Drew, will be here directly. From what I've observed since his arrival, he's a well-behaved lad, though perhaps a little quiet, but under the circumstances...." The door opened, and a maid escorted Drew into the room. "Ah, here he is."

Drew glanced around the room, and the boy's face lit up when his gaze fell upon Tremain. The child ran to him, hugging him tightly around the waist.

Without thinking, Tremain smoothed his hair, patting his head gently. "There now, come and meet your governess, Drew."

The lad lifted his head, then looked at her inquisitively.

"This is Miss Eliza Winston, your governess. Miss Winston, Master Drew Payne."

Eliza's smiled and took two steps forward, then crouched down so she would be at Drew's level. "I'm very pleased to meet you. The vicar has told me many wonderful things about you. I'm nervous about being in a new house and position. Do you think you could escort me around and show me everything?" She held out her hand in invitation.

Drew stared at it, then slipped his small hand into hers. "I know where everything is, Miss Winston."

"Drew has made himself at home," Tremain said. "And I'm glad of it. The viscount will be pleased to hear of it."

"I've never been in such a big place. It's like a castle. And everyone is nice. And look at my new clothes, Vicar!"

A rush of warmth moved through him at Drew's happy voice. The brown woolen vest, jacket, and trousers fit the boy well. He made a mental note to instruct Jon to make further purchases.

"You look every inch a fine young gentleman. Show Miss Winston about, and I will see you later."

Eliza and Drew departed.

Jon closed the parlor door. "A stunning-looking woman. The shade of her hair—"

"Jon," Tremain warned.

"Like warm golden sunbeams. Miss Winston is beautiful and kind as well. This is the wretched creature you pulled from a snow bank? My God, Trey. And do not stand there and tell me you're not interested. I know you far too well. I observed the sparkle in your eyes and the curve of a slight smile."

"Leave off. I've no intention of involving myself with a woman, and certainly not one under my employ."

Jon crossed his arms and smiled. "Ah, but she doesn't know that. To her, you're the village vicar. A good catch. Watch yourself, my friend, lest you find yourself caught in her net." Jon teased as he often had through their life-long friendship.

"I'm in no condition to enter into a relationship with any woman, however much she appeals."

"Ah. Appeals. I thought as much. Then why did you hire her and bring her to your home?" Jon asked.

A bloody good question.

"Because I don't want her to leave," he answered, his voice soft. "I never could lie to you, Jon. Not in all these years. The sad fact is that I want her like I have never wanted any woman. And I'm in no shape emotionally to handle it."

Jon laid a hand on his shoulder. "It's time you healed, Trey. And you're taking steps to do so with your duties as vicar. But no hard and fast rule says you must do it all alone. You have me. The boy adores you. And so does the governess, I'll wager. Let us in, Trey. Bring us close. The healing process will be all the swifter for it." Jon squeezed his shoulder before letting go. "And when you *are* ready, embrace your family and your title. Live your life and be happy as you deserve."

Tremain sighed. "I will reflect on what you said. Thank you."

Jon stepped back and shrugged. "Well, a good kick in the arse would be as effective. Join me for dinner. The cook whipped up a scrumptious roast of beef. We'll invite your pretty governess and her charge."

Tremain's first instinct was to decline, but what awaited him at home but a bowl of cold stew?

Bring us close.

Not sure he could, but for the sake of their friendship, he could make an effort. It may be time to take that first step. "Very well, dinner. Then I must leave directly after."

Jon slapped him on the back. "There you go. It wasn't hard at all, was it?"

DREW ESCORTED HER TO every room—forty of them, he declared—for he'd explored them. He informed her proudly that the servants did not set up a nursery since he was long past playing with most toys. The child was bright for his age and handsome, with honey-blond locks and clear blue eyes.

The schoolroom was bright and airy, with a chalkboard, bookcases, and a desk for her and one for Drew. A large globe sat by the window, and pencils, mathematical instruments, and notebooks were on the long table by the left wall. Everything needed for her governess duties as the viscount spared no expense.

The more time that they spent together, the more Drew warmed up. It must be overwhelming for him; his mother's passing, coming to live in this place, such changes in a short period. Well, she could certainly relate.

Eliza looked down at Drew and smiled. "Together, we will manage it."

He nodded. "Can we start lessons right now, Miss Winston?"

She glanced at the watch fob pinned to her blouse. "The maid informed me we will join Mr. Dibley and Mr. Colson for dinner. So until then, yes. Where would you like to begin?"

"History!"

Eliza laughed at his enthusiasm.

Two hours later, the maid arrived to escort them to the dining room. Eliza admired the simple elegance of the estate house afresh. The decorations and trimmings were not from another age but reflected the current times with the paneled ceilings, moldings, and cornices. There was no dark wood but instead brightly painted walls or gold wallpaper. Her room took her breath away. Not servants' quarters at all and much fancier than the room she had occupied at her previous employment. She adored the blue-and cream-colored room with white French provincial furnishings.

When they entered the dining room, both men stood. Goodness, she wasn't used to that either. Drew's brows furrowed as he clutched her hand tightly. Good to know she wasn't the only one anxious about this meal. Glancing at the table, Eliza was relieved to see that there was no formal arrangement of six forks and seven spoons. No one sat at the head of the table. Tremain and Mr. Dibley sat side-by-side, so Eliza steered Drew to the opposite.

The footman and maid served the meal, no first and second courses, straight to the meat and potatoes. Drew stared at his plate, either amazed at the amount of food or overwhelmed by the whole situation.

"Don't you like roast beef and potatoes, Drew?" Tremain asked.

"I've never had them, not like this, Vicar."

"Well then, enjoy. But first, since it *is* Sunday, let us bow our heads and give thanks. Bless, O Father, for thy gifts before us. Amen."

Tremain lifted his head and gave her a searing look. A roll of molten heat trickled down her spine. Only he could make a simple prayer of grace sound sensual.

The meal tasted delicious, and the conversation was informal and friendly. From what Eliza gathered, Mr. Dibley and Tremain had known each other a long time, but when she inquired how and from where they were suspiciously vague.

Considering his previous circumstances, Drew was more than able to look after himself. Although Eliza observed his table manners needed polishing, instruction on polite conversation would also be sensible since he interrupted the men twice. With the meal at an end, she stood as did Tremain and Mr. Dibley.

"I think Drew can find his way back to his room. Would you remain a moment, Miss Winston?" Tremain asked.

"Join me in the study before you leave, Vicar." Mr. Dibley stated, then followed Drew into the hallway.

Tremain turned to face her. "I would suggest a walk outside, but it's still too cold. Perhaps you will join me as I walk about the hallways? I need to stretch my leg."

"Of course," she replied. Taking the vicar's arm, they headed down the long hallway at a leisurely pace.

"Do you like the house?" Tremain asked.

"I do. For an estate, it's very cozy and livable, a comfortable place to rusticate during the winter months. I'm surprised the viscount doesn't use it as such."

"The viscount travels a great deal. He's out of the country taking in warmer climes. I'm gratified you like it."

"There are no portraits about. What does Viscount Hawkestone look like, I wonder. Has he ever been here? None of the staff has ever met him."

Tremain stiffened, the muscles under her touch tightening. How curious.

"The Duke of Gransford and some of the family were here about eight years ago. It's one of the lesser properties," Tremain said, his voice low. "The viscount has not been here since being given the title."

"My, to be so rich that this is considered a 'lesser property.' Not that it is any of my business, but shouldn't his lordship be in the House of Lords representing this district instead of traveling to warmer climes and—never mind. It isn't my business. By all accounts, he looks after much through you and Mr. Dibley. I have an annoying habit of speaking my mind."

"Don't ever change," he murmured. "Besides, the house isn't sitting right now. The viscount only recently came into the title. I am certain he will settle here once he completes his travels. He is very involved in the running of this estate."

Eliza silently admonished herself for talking about the viscount in such a way. After all he had done for Drew—and her? Her curiosity will get her in trouble one of these days. Best to change the subject.

"The gardens are not as formal as I thought they would be," Eliza said, pointing out the window. "As you said, the viscount is never here. A shame, the grounds have potential."

"Here, let us go outside." She took his arm as he led them through a side door into a small garden area. "There are plenty of shrubs," Tremain said, pointing toward the path ahead. "But I agree, more could be done. I'm certain once his lordship settles here, he will address it. Let Mr. Dibley know. He will add it to the list."

"Oh, I would never make such a forward request," she murmured. "Although, I suppose I already did in offering my opinion."

He patted her hand gently. "You're a member of the household. Suggest it for the lad. Once the weather improves, lessons can move outdoors. You should have a pleasant garden area in which to use."

"Very well, I shall."

"I do some gardening," Tremain said as they strolled by a cluster of boxwood shrubs.

"Really? What kind?"

"I started a small kitchen garden with parsley, sage, mint, and chamomile. Last year, I planted azaleas. They are my mother's favorite. Gardening gives me a brief respite of tranquility, and it reminds me of home. You look surprised."

She was. Tremain *gardens*. Picturing him kneeling in the dirt, planting his mother's favorite flowers, warmed her heart. What a delightful discovery. And how gratifying he gave little glimpses into his private life.

"I've never done any gardening, not even a window box. I want to try. Will you show me when the weather grows warmer?" Eliza asked, her tone hopeful. They circled and headed inside again.

"If you like."

"Perhaps I should ask Mrs. Tompkins to teach me basic cooking skills. I did assist her more than once in the preparation of meat pies. But I don't have enough confidence to try one alone."

Tremain scoffed. "You? No confidence? I can hardly believe it. The nuns didn't teach you that at the orphanage?"

"No. I wish I had insisted. I only know of a few nursery dishes. I can make pap. Lucky me, it is only bread and milk. Easy enough to do," Eliza chuckled.

"I believe Drew is too old for that particular dish," Tremain teased.

"Speaking of Drew, do you wish him to attend Sunday services?"

"I'll write the viscount and inquire, but until I receive a response, let's start him once a month. I already know your views on religion. Will it be a hardship for you to accompany the boy?"

Eliza laughed. "None at all. All part of my duties. But don't be surprised if I seem preoccupied. Perhaps I will stare at *you*."

"Hmm. Maybe you should not attend. You would distract me from *my* duties."

Eliza stopped and stared up at him. "Would I? Truly? That's one of the nicest things you've ever said to me. Feel free to compliment me again. Soon."

A smile curved about his lips. "Are you teasing me?"

"There, a full-on smile. I've waited close to two weeks to see it. My, Vicar. You *are* a stunningly handsome man, and the smile is merely the icing on a particularly enticing cake."

They started walking again. "Not only a tease but a flirt," Tremain murmured.

She squeezed his arm affectionately. "And you like it."

Tremain grasped her elbow and pulled her into the nearby room, kicking the door shut with his boot. He leaned her against the wall, standing barely an inch apart. "I do like it. I like *you*. But going forward, we should not be alone."

Eliza's heart fluttered like the wings of a bird trying to escape a closed room. "Alone? Like we are now? Why?"

"Because I will want to do this." He captured her lips with his. His cane clattered to the floor as he placed his hands flat against the door on either side of her head. Then he did something that seized her breath: he pressed his body against hers. Eliza instinctively spread her legs under her wool skirt, allowing him to rock his hips forward.

There.

Tremain's erection slid against her, stirring the flames. Though layers of clothes lay between them, the movements created a fervent heat, mimicking the thrusts of sex. He was so wonderfully hard. All over. Solid, all that was masculine.

Yes.

Soft moans escaped from the corner of her mouth. Tremain's kiss deepened and grew more savage and demanding; his hips pressed against her more urgently. Eliza's mind swirled, her heart beating rapidly, her breathing shallow. A deep moan left Tremain.

But then he pushed away from her, and the loss of his hard, muscular body made an ache settle between her legs. With a grumble, he picked up his cane and leaned on it.

"Don't stop," she whispered huskily.

"*This* is why we cannot be alone. It won't happen again." With evident frustration, he ran his hand through his hair and turned from her.

Eliza could not understand why this exasperating man fought the attraction pulsating between them. But she felt he would withdraw further if she pushed him into more at this particular moment.

Another time, another place.

She could be patient.

"Shall we continue on our walk?" Eliza asked sweetly.

Tremain gave her an incredulous look. "Not as yet. For reasons you can well guess."

Since he made the invite, she allowed her gaze to slide below his waist. His arousal was plain to see, straining against his trousers. Seeing it was enough to stir the flames of desire to an almighty heat. Their passion would be well matched.

"Eliza."

She glanced up, giving him an entirely innocent look and batting her eyelashes. "Yes?"

"Tease," he muttered, his voice husky and sensual.

"Shall we talk about you and your church?"

Tremain blinked, seemingly confused at the sudden shift in mood and conversation. "Why?"

"If anything takes your mind off—you know."

"Very well. Though a priest in the Anglican Church, I'm not of an Evangelical bent though it is the current fashion. I'm not severe in my faith nor hold a puritanical zeal concerning my religion. My sermons are short and to the point as I try to avoid overt preaching. Though I believe in God, my belief does not rule my life."

"You are quite different from anyone in the clergy I've ever met. My experience included dour, disciplined nuns and arrogant, judgmental Catholic priests."

Tremain leaned against the back of the sofa. Eliza noticed he kept his right leg outstretched. "Not all in the Catholic Church are as you describe."

She smiled. "I know. Many truly believed in helping those less fortunate. However, my memories are overwhelmed by those wielding a thrashing stick. At least, that was the case for me at St. Ann's. Perhaps it *is* better elsewhere. I have only my own experience to go by."

Tremain slowly rubbed his leg. The poor man must be in pain. "Unfortunately, you find that in every institution and orphanage regardless of who runs it. It's why Drew's mother remained adamant that he not wind up there. I gave her my word. Ruth had experienced much as you did, but judging by her stories—decidedly worse."

Her ordeal could have been much worse. Petty of her to complain. "That poor woman."

"Ruth didn't have an easy life. Being a priest, people tell me many things, especially when dying. Drew is the result of a rather brutal rape. The familiar story of the lord of the house dragging the maid out to the stables and having his way with her—as he believed was his right. When her pregnancy became noticeable, the family tossed her onto the streets. Or so I assume. A story I'm sure you're familiar with since you worked for an earl."

"Yes. Luckily, I'm not with child, nor was I raped. But the story is very familiar all the same. Did she ever reveal who the father is?"

Tremain gave a brisk nod. "She did. I'll keep her confidence on that score. As it is, I have revealed far more than I should, but I wanted you to know what Drew is up against and what his background is. The father is a member of the peerage. A prominent one at that."

"Wait. The father isn't Viscount Hawkestone, is it? Is that why he has taken an interest in the child?"

Tremain's eyes widened in shock as if he had never contemplated that scenario. "No! He didn't know of Drew's existence until I wrote to him and asked for his assistance. I wrote months ago when Ruth Payne first became ill."

As she suspected. More proof Tremain's heart existed. "Shouldn't this unnamed aristocrat be made to at least support Drew financially?" Eliza asked.

"No. The man is an absolute reprobate, and Drew should not be subjected to his acquaintance in *any* form. Let the boy believe his father is long dead. Better that than a bastard son of the aristocracy. You will not tell Drew any of this?"

Eliza shook her head vigorously. "No. Never. I agree with everything you've said. However, others will come to the same conclusion about Drew's parentage. There will be talk."

Tremain winced as he stood. "Then we must do all we can to discourage such gossip and to protect him from it. Well, I think I'm ready to show myself. Let us continue on our walk."

After she opened the door, Eliza slipped her arm through Tremain's, pulling herself closer than she should. Pleased he didn't flinch from her nearness, they continued on their walk. Eliza tumbled a little in love with her frozen vicar in that moment of quiet contemplation.

Chapter 13

BEFORE THE BATTLE BROKE out, Tremain remembered hearing that two lieutenants—one from the Royal Engineers—were in charge and leading the defense of the mission station. How successful was another question.

All around him, there was chaos. Though his head swam in a fever fog, and his eyesight was blurry, he'd be damned if he'd go down without a fight. Thrusting his rifle forward, he stabbed madly with its bayonet, hoping to bury it in an enemy warrior. Judging from the yells and the coppery odor of blood that filled his nostrils, he did. Some even sprayed on his cheeks in the melee. The fight quickened his pulse and temporarily cleared his senses. He parried a Zulu spear thrust and countered with a rifle butt to the man's jaw sending splinters of bone, teeth, and blood in all directions.

The fire was spreading. Tremain could smell burning straw, wood, and, sickeningly, human flesh.—Rifle shots. War cries. The gurgling breath of dying men. Screams of burning men. A horrifying cacophony and images jolted through his consciousness like some devastating, intermittent electric shock.

Though he was a captain, he remained unable to lead due to his festering leg injury and high fever. Regardless, he had several moments of incredible clarity. Lucid enough to be aware they all were in danger—and enough to kill the enemy.

A familiar voice came through the smoke and haze. "It's Private Williams, sir. Best come with me. I hacked a hole in the wall. In you go!"

Tremain was shoved through and tumbled into the next room. He couldn't tell how many men were there, but the room was as chaotic as the one he'd just left.

Two men pulled him to his feet and pushed him onto an empty cot. Between the yells and rifle shots, he heard a steady thumping. Is Williams digging another hole? Sweat rolled down his face, and things became hazier. The sounds all blended as the room spun madly about. Where was his rifle?

Frantically he reached all around him until he felt the stock. Twisting to grab it, a rush of air brushed his cheek. He barely missed a spear thrust. In a fevered rage, he dropped his rifle, clasped his hands around the neck of the Zulu who tried to kill him and squeezed with all his strength and fear he could muster. Something in the Zulu's throat popped.

With a sudden burst of energy, he began to pummel his enemy's face until he heard bones crack and blood run down his closed fists. He absently picked a tooth from one of his knuckles—

TREMAIN AWOKE, SHOCKED to find that he was beating his pillow. He had battered it so fiercely he'd punched a hole in it, and feathers floated around him. Sweat ran into his eyes and mixed with angry, frustrated tears. Fear had raised his skin in cold and clammy gooseflesh.

Jesus.

What if there had been a woman in his bed? What if it had been Eliza? He would have beaten her bloody without even being aware of it. His stomach lurched, and he hung his head over the side of the bed and vomited.

Wiping his mouth, Tremain flopped back on a mass of tangled sheets. He'd ripped those as well. Though the nightmares had somewhat lessened over the past two years, they were as intense and real as ever. Would he *ever* get past this? Once he'd recovered from his leg wound, Tremain bought out his commission and took a solemn vow: to banish the horrors of war, to pay penance for the men he'd killed, Tremain would embrace the career that he turned his back on years before and become a member of the clergy.

At first, his father, the duke, was shocked at this change in direction, but both parents supported him, as did Spencer and Harrison. They allowed him the time he needed to heal. Thus the false story of staying in the Mediterranean to recover. His family had also agreed, though reluctantly, to keep their distance for at least two years. The time was up. Still, he felt dead inside.

Except when in Eliza's presence.

Exhaling, Tremain ran his hands through his damp hair. The walk in the garden earlier had disturbed him. A sharp pain tore through him, and not from his mangled leg. The lies were piling up and weighing heavy. When Eliza had brought up the viscount, it would have been the perfect opportunity to reveal his true identity. He wasn't ready. Luckily, his family's visit to the Hawkestone estate eight years ago did not include him. He was away, fighting in the Ashanti war.

And what about her asking if Hawkestone was Drew's father? By God, the possibility had never crossed his mind. However, once revealed to be the viscount, it would be obvious he had *not* sired the boy. Besides the different colors of hair and eyes, they looked nothing alike. Tremain growled and tossed the ruined pillow to the floor.

War. Though he was no longer on the battlefield, a war raged inside him. A battle for his very soul.

If this night terror proved anything, it showed he was far from ready to take up his former life. Last night, for a brief period, he thought he could. He flirted, smiled, and allowed the fantasy to flourish that he could find pleasure and peace in the arms of Eliza Winston. A good thing he had regained control over his passion before they had sex against the door.

Grabbing another pillow, he stuffed it behind his head and drifted into light sleep and dreams of another sort. More pleasant. Much more agreeable.

Eliza walked toward him with a sensual smile and lay on the bed. Spreading her legs, he knelt in between them.

He lay on his stomach, wrapping his arms around her thighs and spread her wide, then plunged his tongue inside her. Eliza writhed and moaned, grasping a handful of his hair while bucking her hips—a sweetly agonizing climax.

Tremain cracked open his eyes to find himself alone in the room. Hard and aroused, he stroked his shaft while reliving the erotic dream, every slide of his tongue, every soft moan. In his past life, Tremain enjoyed oral foreplay, tasting his various lovers until they came apart under his tongue. With a husky yell, he reached his peak. The climax was so intense that he shuddered for several minutes. His wounded leg grew taut, causing his eyes to water from the brief but intense agony.

Pleasure and pain.

It certainly encompassed his feelings for Eliza. Feelings he must keep to himself.

Friends.

It was all they could ever be.

Tremain cared far too much for Eliza to subject her to his terrors. Subject her to the man who held no control during his nightmares. To the man who could harm her.

And that would destroy him utterly.

FOR THREE WEEKS, ELIZA tried to get Tremain alone. When she did see him, he was more polite than usual but with a detached civility, as if he'd learned a new way to contain his emotions around her. The coldness had receded, but Tremain replaced it with a polite indifference she found nearly as disturbing as his former frosty demeanor.

The man continued to infuriate her, and perhaps a lesser woman would have walked away, finding him not worth the effort. But in the past several weeks, she had enough of a glimpse to understand that he not only suffered physically but in his soul.

Damaged.

To what extent, she still needed to ascertain.

Meanwhile, Eliza settled into the ebb and flow of Hawkestone Estate. It was an informal and relaxed atmosphere compared to her previous position in Yorkshire. The small staff had offered friendship, inviting her to dinner below stairs several times a week. She accepted gladly and gratefully. There was also the once-a-week dining with Mr. Dibley, Tremain, and Drew.

Jon Dibley was an attractive man, three or four inches taller than her, with coffee-colored hair and a closely-trimmed beard. However, his pleasant looks and amiable manner were not enough to entice her. Beyond Tremain's dark handsomeness, she sensed that he needed her. Leave it to her to fall for the damaged, tortured man.

Perhaps they needed each other.

Eliza became firmly convinced they could fill the hole in each other's hearts. This realization made her even more committed to breaching Tremain's defenses. Why not a vicar and a governess? They would make an exciting couple, though being a vicar's wife held no appeal in the religious sense. For his sake, she could attempt it. Shaking her head and dismissing the fanciful daydreams, Eliza turned her attention to Drew. They were studying the War of the Roses when a knock sounded at the door.

Tremain stepped in. Drew glanced up, his face shining in happiness. Tremain returned the smile, though briefly, and patted the lad affectionately on the head. He cared for Drew, and observing the genuine fondness between man and boy made her heart tumble.

"Drew has a request, Vicar," she said.

"What is it, lad?"

"Well, I liked the meat pies Miss Winston brought from the pub, and I wonder if we all could go for lunch there, maybe tomorrow? Or next week?"

Tremain caught Eliza's gaze over the top of Drew's head, giving her a suspicious look. Though an excellent plan, she could not lay claim to it. It was all Drew's idea.

"Miss Winston, may I speak to you briefly in the hall?"

"Of course. Drew, please read the next five pages, and when I return, I will quiz you on them. We will also have an answer from the vicar, I promise."

Tremain clutched her arm and pulled her none too gently from the room, closing the door behind him. "What is your game?" he whispered, his teeth clenched.

"Oh, come now. Do you think I put the child up to this? How devious do you think I am? It was *his* suggestion. Not mine," she sniffed. How dare he accuse her?

Leaning on his cane, he slapped his free hand against the wall beside her. "Listen to me carefully, Eliza. I cannot be seen with a member of my parish in a social situation, particularly a pretty governess who tempts me beyond all endurance." Tremain shook his head. "I cannot be involved with you, or it will be just cause for my dismissal. For all intents and purposes, I am a priest in the Anglican Church, and certain rules must be adhered to."

"Have you taken a vow of celibacy?"

"No, of course not. But decrees are in place, and I'm honor-bound to obey them. And I shall."

Well. How convenient. The first time Tremain has mentioned this.

"I'm not a member of your parish," Eliza said matter-of-factly. "I was going to attend the service this Sunday, but I'll stay here instead. Mr. Dibley can accompany Drew to church. There. Problem solved."

Tremain pushed away from the wall, backing up several steps. "Whether you attend services or not, you *live* in my parish. It's a small village, and people talk. I'm sure the hens are clucking already over our proximity. I would rather avoid scandal if it is all the same to you. My work here is not done, and I..." He clamped his mouth shut.

"What work? Your duties as a vicar?"

He shook his head. "Never mind. No lunch in the village."

Obstinate man.

"You would break that poor boy's heart? He talks of you constantly. He absolutely adores you. Do not push him away because you cannot stand to be in my presence."

Tremain walked toward her purposefully, the cane thumping loudly against the wood floor. "I want nothing more than to be in your presence." He stopped mere inches from her and stroked her cheek with his fingers. Eliza shuddered at his touch; how she had missed it. As her insides rolled and dipped, a ragged groan escaped her lips.

Leaning in, he whispered in her ear. "I want nothing more than to be inside you, thrusting deep until I come. Until *you* come. Preferably at the same time." Eliza raised her hands to clutch his coat and pull him closer, but he'd already stepped away. "But it won't happen. I won't allow it." His voice was hoarse, with need perhaps? It was hard to say, as his face remained unreadable and resolute.

Collecting herself, she cleared her throat. "It's only lunch at a pub. I'm not suggesting a torrid dalliance, though the idea holds merit considering your wicked words. Say yes to Drew. I promise I'll stay far away and not even look at you. We will be all that is proper."

"Blast it all. This is not a game. This is my livelihood that you mock, my calling." He turned away, and shame coursed through her. In trying to recreate the teasing flirtation they'd shared three weeks ago, she managed to make a fool of herself and insult him.

"Forgive me. You're correct. This is *not* a game. We must stop goading each other like this. Why did you allow the viscount to offer me employment if I am such a-a-a—"

"Attractive woman? A distraction that haunts my dreams?"

Eliza flushed with pleasure at his words. "I'll inform Drew that you're busy and cannot attend."

"Oh, blast. The day after next, we'll go to the village in my wagon. For lunch. Then I'll bring you both straight back here." Tremain turned to face her. "But you understand we cannot take this attraction any further?"

"Yes. I understand," Eliza answered contritely. But she would not give up. After this conversation, Eliza became all the more convinced that they needed each other.

Chapter 14

ADMONISHING HIMSELF for weakening and agreeing to this luncheon engagement took up part of Tremain's time during the next forty-eight hours. But, as the three of them sat in the wagon heading toward Hawksgreen, Tremain dismissed the thoughts and, for once, would make an effort to enjoy the day.

The lingering snow from the late January storm had almost melted, and since it was the first week in March, a distinct smell of spring loitered in the air. With the sporadic birdsong came a promise of renewal and rebirth. He should take a lesson from nature and allow seeds to grow.

What seeds exactly?

The words Jon spoke to him some weeks back had never left his mind. They had taken root. At this time, he still did not feel he could enter into a complicated relationship with Eliza, but why not enjoy each other's company, however innocently? Besides, he was fond of Drew. Last week, Tremain had instructed Jon to contact the solicitor. Although Tremain could just take the boy into his home without any legal ramifications, he wanted paperwork on file for his peace of mind.

In the meantime, Tremain continued his duties as vicar. Since the village and its surrounding farms constituted a small area, he had a good deal of leisure time on his hands. He made the expected rounds, sitting in parlors while the lady of the house asked, "More tea, Vicar?" He also visited places no better than hovels.

Tremain had donated small amounts of food during his tenure. The poorer parishioners, though proud in bearing, had accepted his gifts with gratitude. He would also provide seed later in the spring to impoverished farmers and lumber for repairs on behalf of his viscount counterpart. All these altruistic acts assisted in healing his tortured soul, but more importantly, the gifts aided those in need.

Tremain started a journal of everything he'd witnessed as vicar and during the war: the iniquitousness of society and the wretched poverty. Interacting with a vast swath of classes had opened his eyes to the plight of those less fortunate. There was much to report to his father. As the Duke of Gransford, his father held power within the aristocracy that could see things done. As the second son and a viscount in his own right, Tremain also could advocate for fair treatment to people experiencing poverty, as Jon had pointed out. As could Harrison, as the Marquess of Tennington.

All this brought the looming specter of his future into sharp focus. When he became a vicar, he had no intention of keeping the position for the rest of his life. He understood his place in society and within his own family, and even if he wished for a career with the church, being a country vicar was not the anticipated path of a duke's second son. He would be expected to become a clergyman in a prominent church in London with ambitions to become a bishop, beholden to rich and titled patrons, and that prospect did *not* appeal to Tremain in any way. It was one of the main reasons he didn't enter the church after graduating from Cambridge.

It was all a moot point, as he could not keep up this dual life much longer. He, at last, had come to that conclusion. Finding a suitable recently ordained young man to take his place would be the first step, and then he would be honor bound to fulfill his role as Viscount Hawkestone. As Jon advised, he could accomplish much as a viscount rather than a vicar.

Tremain glanced at Eliza sitting beside him, her hand resting gently on his arm. Drew sat on the other side, chattering away about his lessons. He felt at peace with this lovely lady and the young lad. How would they respond when they discovered he had lied to them about his identity? How would the village react? Jon brought up that salient point when Tremain had first informed him of his plan. Ultimately, he'd dismissed the concerns, which would be dealt with later.

The thing is, that *later time* drew near.

The village came into view. Many people were out and about since it was such a pleasant early spring day. Tremain cursed inwardly. It would create all the more opportunity for the few busybodies to see him with Eliza. Under the circumstances, he would have to try to shutter his emotions more than usual.

Once the carriage was seen to, Jonas Tompkins escorted them to one of his best tables. It sat in the corner beside the fireplace, with a half wall offering a modicum of privacy.

"Now, what can I get you all?" Jonas smiled.

"Meat pies!" Drew said eagerly.

"Meat pies all around. Tea for Miss Winston and myself and a large glass of fresh milk for Drew," Tremain stated.

"Very well, Vicar. And Drew, Mrs. Tompkins has a special treat. She made a chocolate cake. Would you like a piece for dessert?"

Drew gazed up at Tremain expectantly, his eyes wide and pleading. The boy insisted on sitting next to him, and he had to admit that Drew's open and honest adoration warmed him. "Absolutely. Cake for all."

The conversation between them was easy and friendly as they waited for the food. A few patrons whispered behind their hands. Tremain observed that they attracted attention. Blast it all, but what did it matter at the end of the day? Try as he might, he couldn't act the cold vicar today; he was too bloody happy.

The food arrived, and Tremain cut into the meat pie, popping a piece in his mouth. He caught Eliza's gaze, her emerald eyes sparkling prettily at him. His heart thumped madly in response. Yes, masking his emotions was becoming more difficult by the moment.

As they sat at the table sharing a meal, Tremain could admit that he yearned for a family. He longed to have a strong, attractive, and intelligent woman by his side to share his duties by day and his bed by night. A son he could be proud of, honorable and compassionate toward humanity—the secret desires of any decent, stable man.

However, he was not stable.

Though he acknowledged, the healing had begun. And decent? It could be argued. After Tompkins took away the empty plates, he sat generous slices of cake before them.

"Oh, how sinfully delicious this looks," Eliza said.

Tremain could not tear his eyes from her as she lifted a piece of cake toward her sensual mouth. Sweat broke out at his hairline when she licked the fork, her dainty tongue dashing away a spot of frosting from her bottom lip. Even watching her eat aroused him.

When they finished, Tremain paid the innkeeper, and they all thanked the Tompkinses profusely for the delicious meal. They stepped outside. Across the road, four young lads played tag. Drew watched them intently.

"Do you know those boys, Drew?" Eliza asked.

"They're my mates."

Eliza laid a hand on his shoulder. "Go and say hello. The vicar and I will take a short walk."

Drew gave her a brilliant smile and scampered off toward the other boys. Tremain offered her his arm, and she took it.

"He must be lonely at the estate with no one to play with. Every child should have a friend," Eliza stated.

"Very true. Unfortunately, life sometimes makes it difficult to form attachments."

"Speaking from your own experience? Aren't you and Mr. Dibley long-time friends?"

"Yes."

Eliza squeezed his arm. "You never talk about him, your family, or your past. Was it so horrible?"

"Quite the opposite. I had a wonderful childhood. And I have a wonderful family. While I can boast a large circle of acquaintances, I only have a few I would call friends. My two brothers and Jon. And *you*, Miss Eliza Winston."

So much for shuttering my emotions.

When he spoke her name, his tone hid nothing. It held all his yearnings and desires for affection. Companionship. And Eliza heard it, for she pulled closer to him and sighed, her hand caressing his sleeve. Again, heated sparks flew between them.

Time to change the subject before he revealed more of his turbulent emotions.

"I've received a response from the housekeeper in Yorkshire. She confirmed your story, background, and experience," Tremain said.

"So, you believe me?"

"Eliza, I've always believed you. I wrote the letter to ensure that I can offer proof if anyone questions your abilities and qualifications. I regret to inform you that she adamantly refuses on behalf of Lady Bowater to replace the money and reference stolen from you, even though they employ the brutes who had perpetrated the crimes."

Eliza laughed cynically. "So much for any justice, as I assume those men are still under her employ, not that I expected any. How—"

Loud voices broke into their conversation. The boys had chased Drew back across the lane.

"Leave off, you toff. You be too high and mighty to be with the likes of us," one boy yelled at Drew.

Another picked up a handful of mud and threw it toward Drew, but he nimbly jumped out of the way. "Go back to yer 'igh and mighty viscount. We don't want yer type round 'ere."

"Oh, Tremain," Eliza gasped.

He strode across the street as fast as his wretched leg would allow. Protectively, he placed his arm around Drew. "Be off, the lot of you!"

The boys scattered, running off in different directions. Crouching down, he turned Drew to face him. The boy's lower lip trembled, and his eyes were moist, but he did not cry. Tremain's heart swelled with sympathy.

Taking Drew and placing him at the estate may have been a selfish move on his part—another of many selfish actions. He thrust the boy into a world he knew nothing about, and those he'd left behind would never let him forget it.

Drew threw his arms about his neck. "I'm all right, Vicar. It will be all right."

Tremain hugged him back, and a surge of emotion gripped him tight. To hell with making this boy his ward. Instead, he would give him his name—if Drew wanted it. He loved this child as if he were his own.

"Yes. It will be all right, Drew. You'll see."

"Can we stop and visit my mother's grave on the way home?" he asked, his voice soft and shaky.

"Of course, lad. We shall."

Ten minutes later, the three of them stood before the resting place of Ruth Payne on the church property. "Mr. Dibley informed me the stone is on order. The viscount approved it," Tremain said solemnly.

Drew slipped his hand in Tremain's. "Will I meet The Hawk—I mean, the viscount soon?"

"Yes, lad. Sooner than you might suppose." Eliza shot Tremain a puzzled look, but he ignored it.

"It doesn't matter that my mates don't like me anymore," Drew said quietly.

"You can make new friends when you go off to school in a year or so," Eliza assured him.

"Yes, I have all the friends I need now: you, the vicar, Mr. Dibley, Anna, and the cook, Mrs. Hughes. I want to learn. I *want* to go away to school." He gazed up at Tremain. "I want to be a doctor so people like my mum have proper care. I want to help cure diseases and help the sick. Can I do that, Vicar?"

A lump of emotion lodged in Tremain's throat. "My dear boy, you can do anything you put your mind to. Medicine is a fine profession. The Hawk will be proud. *I* am proud. We'll see it done. Miss Winston will do all she can to prepare you to achieve your goal." He glanced at Eliza, who nodded as she swiped away a tear. At that moment, Tremain never cared for two people more.

And he did not deserve it.

Chapter 15

ELIZA DECIDED TO CONFRONT Tremain and take their budding relationship further, if indeed they would have any relationship at all. Perhaps it was arrogant of her to assume Tremain would welcome her bold advances, but as time passed, it became clear she would have to approach him. The signs were there that he cared far more than he had let on. She had to know how he felt about her and if it could be more than the friendship he'd mentioned.

Stubborn man.

Most women in her shoes would've given up, but something compelled her forward.

The man was annoyingly vague about his life and past, as if he were keeping a secret. Besides his obvious physical attributes, she found him complex, mysterious, brooding, and utterly passionate and compassionate, though he tried to hide it at every turn. Was he keeping a secret? Watching him interact with Drew during their outing that afternoon had touched her.

Frozen heart indeed. What a fallacy.

Gathering her courage, she waited until Drew was fast asleep and the other occupants of Hawkestone Estate were otherwise engaged, put on her cloak, then exited the manor house through the kitchen door and walked to the vicarage. She clasped the key in her cloak pocket, a way to get back inside should all the doors be locked after a particular hour.

The full moon cast enough light to find her way. Eliza's heart fluttered madly with each step. This plan could be a terrible mistake and could damage what little progress they've made.

No one wants to be rejected.

However, the memory of his heated, passionate kisses and wicked and arousing words urged her onward.

A light burned in the corner window, but the rest of the residence was dark. Good God, had he retired for the night? With a cleansing breath, she rapped on the door. Eliza could hear the familiar sound of his cane thumping against the wood planks. The door opened.

"Yes, who is it?"

Eliza lowered the hood of her cloak and met his gaze. He wore black trousers and a white shirt that lay halfway down his torso. Seeing the strong column of his neck, and the teasing glimpse of chest hair, made her swallow hard. Tremain was temptation itself. Tremain had rolled up his shirtsleeves showing corded, muscular forearms, and ink stains were visible on two of his fingers. No doubt he'd been working in his study.

"Eliza. Has something happened?" he asked worriedly.

"No, everyone is fine." She gave him a shaky smile.

"Then, what—" Tremain pulled her across the threshold, closing the door. "Someone could have seen you," he admonished sternly.

"At nine o'clock? I rather doubt it. Early to bed, early to rise, is what people around here live by. I treasure my time in the latter part of the evening. Do you?"

Tremain leaned on his cane. "Why are you here?"

Yes, why?

Nerves caused her hands to tremble, as she might be about to make a severe miscalculation. Unbuttoning her cloak, it fell to the floor, and she stood before Tremain wearing nothing but her corset and skirt. The undergarment was her best, lowcut with lace, exposing her cleavage to its best advantage. Surely it would get a reaction.

Or perhaps not.

He stood as still and stony as a sandstone statue. Yet looking into the depths of his silver-gray eyes, heat emanated from them instead of his usual frosty gaze.

"Do you take a twisted delight in tempting me? Are you cruel to your core?" he whispered.

Eliza's heart dropped to her toes. Even though her first instinct was to flee, she heard desire in his tone. She'd known him long enough to recognize it. Gathering her courage, she stepped closer and laid a hand flat against his chest. His heart banged furiously under her touch.

"No, Tremain. I'm not here to torment you. Far from it. I'm here to seduce you. Shocking, isn't it? Try as I might, I cannot stay away."

An agonized moan left his throat as he awkwardly backed away, causing him to stumble and crash to the floor. Eliza cried out and rushed to his side. Tremain struggled to his feet, groaning with the effort.

"You wish to seduce a cripple?" he roared. "Go back to the manor house, Miss Winston. There's nothing here for you!"

A raw fury tore through her veins, making her blood boil. "You wretch, how dare you? Do you know what it took for me to come here tonight? You are a stubborn man. I desire you, though I've no idea why, considering your gloomy, taciturn demeanor." Eliza stood close, poking him in the chest. "Then you let the mask down enough to allow a brief glimpse of the passionate man beneath. You. Torture. Me. And I don't care if you have a disability."

He grabbed her wrist. "You'd care if you saw the injury. It's vile, and I would not subject any woman to suffer it, especially not you."

Eliza pulled her arm from his grip. "Are you in pain?"

Tremain grimaced. "I'm always in pain."

"Do you take a nostrum, perhaps laudanum, or morphine?"

"No. I tried laudanum while recovering in the hospital, but I despised the false feeling of euphoria. The doctor who treated me was himself addicted to morphine. I wanted no part of any narcotic that would wield such control over me." He paused, then frowned. "I've come to believe that if a man is in pain—it serves to remind him of his mortality. I've made a friend of my pain." As he spoke, he rubbed his leg.

"Then let me help you. One thing that I learned at the orphanage was how to apply a mustard plaster. It will bring modest relief," Eliza urged.

Tremain shook his head. "No, absolutely not. No one has seen my injury except doctors and nurses." He gazed out the parlor window. He said in a soft, low voice, "You've come to seduce me. I've not been with a woman since before the war—more than three years. I'm not sure I can even manage to achieve sex. Not arousal. You've proved I still experience that. I'm speaking of the physical act. Due to the pain in my leg and thigh, I may be unable to perform—Oh, hell."

Eliza took a couple of tentative steps toward him. The moon cast his magnificent profile in soft illumination, his look reflective and vulnerable. She clutched his bare forearm, his skin warm to the touch.

"Then let us see if I can manage well enough. Your disability doesn't disgust me. I'm a strong woman, Tremain. You've said so yourself. Why don't you lay by the fire? I will gather some blankets and pillows for your comfort and apply the plaster to your thigh and leg." Her breasts brushed against his arm, causing him to take a sharp intake of breath. "Do not send me away. Let us see where this will take us."

He nodded, and it took all her control not to react joyfully at his acquiescence. No matter how horrendous his wound was, she could not react, or it would cause him to withdraw deep to a place she may not be able to reach him ever again. As Eliza hurried down the hall toward the guest bedroom to fetch blankets and pillows, she realized the barriers she wished to breach were the ones around his heart and soul. Yes, she cared deeply for him, may even be half in love with him already.

HARD AS A STEEL PIKE—FROM the moment she removed her cloak, her abundant breasts all but spilling over her corset in invitation. Blast it all. It hurt to walk across the room. How could he manage various sex positions? Years ago, Tremain had a reputation as an arduous and capable lover. It reminded him of his recent erotic dream and probably explained his compliance on the mustard plaster—and the vulnerable confession of his doubts about sex. Like the pompous ass he once was, he'd reveled and preened over the compliments. Yes, his life was once that vacuous.

Eliza reentered, carrying a bundle of bedding and pillows. With quick efficiency, she arranged them before the fire.

"Now, do you have mustard seed? Never mind, I'll find it in the kitchen. May I use some towels, or do you have muslin?" He nodded, not able to speak. "Please sit and relax. I will find everything and return directly."

He let his gaze linger as she breezed from the room. Before he sat, he limped to the front door, bolted it, and pulled the curtains closed. Tremain wondered if he was making a grave error. Sooner or later, this situation would crop up, as he did not intend to remain celibate for the remainder of his life. He would rather it be with a woman he cared deeply about rather than a passing liaison.

And he cared for Eliza. Very much.

Examining the breadth and depth of his feelings would merely complicate matters. When he decided to take on the role of vicar, he had no intentions of entering relationships of any kind. Yet, he had allowed Drew and Eliza close. His lies and false identity would eventually hurt them. Anger them enough to turn away from him. How did things become so tangled?

She entered the room carrying a large porcelain bowl. "You haven't removed your trousers."

"Eliza, this is *not* a good idea."

She placed the bowl on the table, then moved toward him. "Nonsense. Here, allow me."

Standing close, the sight of her luxurious golden hair loose and flowing past her shoulders hardened him further. The scent of wildflowers filled his senses.

She unbuttoned his shirt and pushed it past his shoulders until it fell to the floor.

"My, Vicar. You're a fine specimen. I observed it that night long ago when I walked in on you bathing. But to see you up close is a decided treat."

"I've lost weight since the war. I used to be more muscular than this," Tremain whispered, pleased at her admiration.

Eliza gazed up at him. "Truly? You must have been a formidable force on the battlefield." She trailed her fingers down his chest with a soft sigh, leaving burning heat in her wake. She explored him, brushing past his nipples until they hardened, moving up his arms and caressing his biceps. He was putty in her hands and relished the command she was taking over him.

"What's this?" Eliza touched a circular scar on his left shoulder.

"Rifle wound."

"The same time you injured your leg?"

Tremain shook his head. "Two years before. The bullet was nearly spent, and the wound not serious."

"And this scar on your collarbone?"

"Spear. I believe the Zulu warrior was trying to plunge it through my neck. Instead, it grazed the bone."

"The same time you injured your leg?" she whispered.

He nodded. As if sensing he couldn't speak of it, Eliza distracted him by continuing to touch him, this time dipping below the waist. A husky groan tore from his throat when her feather-like stroke explored his hardened length.

Gripping him tight, she stood on her toes and whispered sensually in his ear, "And quite the specimen here as well."

"Oh, God," Tremain groaned. Lost in a lustful haze, he didn't realize she'd unbuttoned his trousers. He froze. "Wait. I don't think—"

Eliza cupped his face, her thumb brushing across his flushed cheek. "Let me see, Tremain."

"It's horrible," he rasped.

There were many times in his life he knew raw fear. Most of the incidents were during his career as a soldier. But what he experienced here nearly rivaled it. Eliza gripped the trousers, and his small clothes, then pushed them downward. No hiding anything now; he stood before her, fully exposed. His blatant arousal proved his desire, his hands clenched into fists showed his reluctance, and his chest rapidly rising and falling confirmed he'd never been as vulnerable.

The injury ran from his upper thigh to his knee. By all rights, he should have lost the entire leg, but mercifully, he recovered from the fever that had gripped him during the Battle of Rorke's Drift, and the limb hadn't turned gangrenous.

"Oh, Tremain," she said, her voice soft. He kept his gaze on her as if defying her to respond with disgust and horror. Instead, Eliza continued her exploration of the indentations across his thigh, and the massive scarring and raw, red skin pulled taut across the damaged muscle. "Can you tell me what happened?"

"A skirmish with a few Zulus. We were on a scouting mission when they came upon our camp at twilight. They are amazingly quiet; I never heard a thing. Since I was not fully asleep, I managed to twist away just as the warrior thrust the spear, grazing my collarbone."

Tremain gulped as he'd never told anyone this before, but he'd come this far. "I managed to stumble to my feet, grabbing my sword simultaneously. Another warrior thrust as I stood, carving my right side as if I were a side of beef. He tried again, this time aiming for my heart. I knocked his spear away with my blade, but not before he sliced my leg again. I turned and ran the first warrior through, killing him. The leg bled profusely while large skin flaps hung to the knee, muscle and tendons exposed. The pain was unbearable, and I collapsed."

He paused and took a deep breath. Exhaling, he met Eliza's gaze. Her eyes were wide, but showed no revulsion. Instead, he saw compassion and concern, which gave him the courage to continue. "I wound up battling the Zulu while rolling around on the ground. The pain clouded my vision, but I managed to grab a large rock and smash him on the head. I kept smashing until his head was nothing more than a pulpy mass of brain and blood. He no longer looked human. I was—am—a beast."

Eliza grasped both his hands and gave them a comforting squeeze. "It was war, Tremain. You were fighting for your life."

"I turned and smashed the head of the warrior I had already killed. I was caught in the throes of bloodlust fueled by excruciating pain. At least, that is what the doctors told me as if to excuse and explain away my brutality. But here's the thing, and this may give you pause to involve yourself any further with me—" Tremain blew out a shaky breath as a tear trickled down his cheek. "I liked it."

Chapter 16

THE WORDS CHILLED ELIZA'S heart. How to respond to such a terrible confession? War was brutal. Though she knew nothing of what men experienced in battle, she imagined it was much as Tremain illustrated. How could it not leave scars, both inside and out?

She gently swiped away his tears. "This is why you became a clergyman? To find peace?"

Tremain took her hand, holding it tight. "Yes. Peace. Forgiveness. Penance. I wanted to give something back to my fellow man, hoping to acquire some relief for my tormented soul. I vowed to try and save men rather than partake of their butchery."

This explanation clarified much of his behavior. But not all of it.

"Are you aware it is spoken in certain circles in the village that you possess a frozen heart?"

A small smile curled about his lips as his thumb brushed the tops of her hand. "I've heard the talk; I encouraged it and even instructed my family to leave me to my own devices since I needed time alone. I wanted no one close. Not easy to achieve when one is a priest. But I believed I could carry out my duties adequately and offer compassion when needed. And I have—in my remote way."

Tremain glanced downward, then continued in a soft voice. "Perhaps I've always lacked that innate warmth. From my earliest memory, I felt separated and distant from everyone. My travails in the Zulu War furthered this coldness to the point where I felt nothing for any individual. I accepted that this was my way. The coldness spread through me and settled into my heart and soul."

"Yet a small boy who lost his mother touched your heart," she whispered.

"And so has an intelligent, strong, and lovely woman whom I found in a snow bank," he replied. Tremain looked at her, his beautiful eyes showing sadness and desire. For all his talk of feeling nothing, she had the distinct impression he felt far too much.

She had always wanted this: sharing one's deepest feelings and fears, being honest and open. Eliza's heart leaped with joy.

"Thank you for telling me about your injury." Tentatively, she ran her fingers across the scarred skin. "I'm not horrified by your wound or what you confessed to me. If your superiors did not hold you accountable for what happened that night, neither should you. Perhaps the time has come to start to forgive yourself." She gave him her warmest smile. "Now, concerning your injury, we should address it immediately. Lie on your side, and I'll fetch the plasters."

He did, and after gathering the bowl, she turned to face him. As he had described, his ghastly injury looked like the warrior had carved him like roast beef. No wonder he lived with constant pain. Kneeling next to him, Eliza met his inquiring gaze. One eye stared at her from the pillow, watching her every move.

"I located pieces of muslin in the linen cupboard. In between the layers, I spread a blend of crushed mustard seed and ginger mixed with flour and water to make a paste. This will feel hot. I'll keep a close watch so it doesn't burn you." Eliza laid the cloth on his thigh, and he took a sharp intake of breath.

Concentrating on her task remained difficult as her gaze slid to Tremain's aroused state more than once. The erection had lessened during his war narrative, but it sprang back to life when she touched him. Grasping another piece of cloth, Eliza laid it against his leg.

Smoothing them out, she said, "The nuns taught me a mustard plaster stimulates blood flow and improves circulation. The warmth will relieve your pain."

"*You* relieve my pain." He clasped her hand and then squeezed as if needing her strength.

"You know, Tremain, if you did not possess a heart or a conscience, your war experiences would not torment you as they do. You would've brushed them off and continued with your life without care. But you didn't. What you told me is dreadful. I cannot imagine how haunted you must be by these terrible experiences. I'm not disgusted, nor do I condemn you. Instead, I'm glad that you survived. You wished to heal. Why else enter the church? Giving back to one's fellow man is noble. I quite admire you."

"I have nightmares," he whispered, his voice husky.

"I'm not surprised, considering what you related to me."

Tremain squeezed her hand tighter. "They're too real. I awoke one morning, pummeling my pillow to shreds. What if that had been you? Do you now understand why we cannot become involved? Why I push you away?" His tone was laced with agony, and her heart flooded with sympathy.

Eliza kissed his forehead. "I do understand. I also comprehend that these nightmares may stay with you for some time, perhaps always. That is why you must seek relief where you can, to lessen them. Ask for support from those who care for you. Reach out to other soldiers. You don't have to do it alone."

"So wise. Thank you. For listening. For caring." His voice was deep, rough with emotion.

"I will listen anytime you wish. You can tell me anything. Now, relax and allow the warmth to flow through you. I'll stay with you as long as you wish."

"You are an amazing woman."

"Another compliment. You're making me blush." Pulling her hand from his, she lifted the plaster and examined his skin. She massaged around his knee, and Tremain moaned. "Pain?"

"No. It feels good. Keep doing it."

The muscles in his leg were tight and knotted. Eliza worked them, kneading and caressing. His eye fluttered shut, and his body relaxed. After inspecting the plasters a second time, she removed them. With a gentle nudge, she pushed Tremain onto his back. She kissed his collarbone without giving him time to react until his eyes snapped open.

"What—"

"Allow me to explore."

Laying on her side next to him, Eliza grasped his hardness, then squeezed, causing a husky moan to reverberate in his powerful chest. "Tell me what to do, Tremain. Please tell me what you want. My brief experience didn't involve touching like this. Instruct me."

"What do I want? I want you to make me come. Stroke me, please. Never stop touching me." His voice was gruff with desire.

"Am I too bold?" She already knew the answer: she was being *very* bold. She never touched a man like this before. How fascinating, hard yet soft.

Tremain shook his head. "Never. I applaud your boldness and courage. Not only overall but in coming here tonight. I was attracted to you from the first but kept my distance because I believed that I did not deserve it. I still believe it. I've acted as a coward. In many ways."

Eliza laid kisses along his chin and cheek. "Not a coward, not in my eyes. You deserve everything. Peace, happiness, contentment, and passion. Allow me to help you achieve it."

As she increased the pace of her strokes, Tremain's moans became deeper. The flickering firelight highlighted every chiseled aspect of his muscled body. The cords in his neck pulled tautly; his sensual lips parted as she explored him. Laying urgent kisses along his collarbone, she moved downward, and he shuddered. Her tongue left no part of him untouched, and when she reached his shaft, she left no part of that unexplored either. Eliza kissed and licked, reveling in his taste. Her mouth closed over the swollen head of his erection.

Tremain groaned. "Yes, more." There was no hiding his feelings now; he was physically and emotionally exposed. Vulnerable. And it touched her, her feelings coming into sharper focus.

With a growl, he gently grabbed a fistful of her hair, holding her still as he thrust deeper into her mouth. Hard to tell if the sounds leaving his throat was mired with pain, lust, or a combination of both. His right leg tensed. Perhaps he was in discomfort. Eliza halted briefly from her ministrations.

"I'm nearly there. A moment more—" With a ragged cry, Tremain pulled away, spilling on the blanket. This was much more intense than what she'd shared with William.

How wondrous.

TREMAIN TREMBLED WITH the force of his release. Good God, he'd never experienced such an intense climax. Eliza smiled, and he pulled her down to rest against his shoulder. His Eliza was a passionate woman.

His Eliza?

Try as he might, he could no longer keep her at a distance, physically or otherwise. She had said as much at the beginning of their acquaintance. How could he deny the powerful force of their attraction?

"I want to pleasure you in return," he said, caressing her arm.

She shook her head. "Not tonight. This was all for you."

"There will be more between us, then?"

"How can we avoid it? Unless I leave. Find another place to settle far from here. Do you want me to leave?" she whispered.

Leave? Initially, yes, if only to protect her.

Now? Never. *Ever.*

But how could this work? His mind raced, not sure how much to reveal. Though he had confessed much to her, plenty remained unspoken.

"No, I don't want you to leave." At least he was honest about this.

Eliza trailed her fingers through his chest hair. "Tremain?"

"Yes?"

"Am I a sinful woman?" she asked, her voice soft and tremulous. "Isn't that what your faith would decree?"

"I thought you didn't subscribe to any religion?"

"I don't. But *you* do. I could not bear to think you believe me to be—what do people call it in your church—a fallen woman?"

The church preached abstinence until marriage. To him, sex was as essential to one's life as food, water, and air. Since becoming a clergyman, he mentioned abstinence to younger parishioners but innately understood desire and love often overrode cautious and prudent thought.

"I don't lay guilt and shame on those who find pleasure with another—as long as it's consensual and they take precautions. As you can imagine, I keep these thoughts to myself, considering the rigidities of Victorian society and the church itself."

Tremain nuzzled her neck and continued, "We're both mature enough to understand the consequences and the possible ramifications. This is why we cannot do more tonight, as I have nothing to use to prevent a child." He shook his head. "A fallen woman? Never. Not to me."

"Good. Because I have sheaths, I insisted that William purchase some before I would agree to the dalliance. He must have had plenty on hand, for he gave me more than a few." Eliza exhaled. "If you wish this to go further, there is protection. I wanted you to know. I had them well hidden in a small locked box. When the staff packed up my trunk in Yorkshire, they tossed the case inside."

"How prudent of you to insist that of him. What happens between us is no one's business but our own. I desire you. More importantly, I respect you. And, regardless of my initial actions, I have—from the first. And yes, as far as taking this further? We can...one day at a time."

She leaned on her elbow and gazed down at him, her eyes moist. "I do wish it. You're a puzzling man. If you were attracted to me from the first, why fight to keep me away? You must have known I reciprocated the feelings. Was it, as you said earlier, you believed you didn't deserve it? Or perhaps concern that you may harm me during your nightmares?"

Tremain cupped her cheek, caressing her chin with the pad of this thumb. "Yes. All that. Especially the harm. I don't want to *hurt* you, Eliza, in any way. Perhaps the time has come to forgive myself for my heinous crimes against humanity. But first. Allow me to apologize for my remoteness. I will strive to do better. With you and the world at large."

"Yes. Forgive yourself, for I forgive you, Tremain. Kiss me?" Eliza gave him a warm and welcoming smile, melting more of the ice surrounding his heart. He would be wholly thawed before the sun rose if they kept up in this direction.

Capturing his mouth with hers, he kissed her deeply. Reverently. As Eliza tunneled her fingers through his hair, he trailed his lips down her throat, finding her pulse point and nibbling on her as if she were a decadent dessert.

Tremain couldn't think of the future or confess his true identity. He had too much else to work out first. Like forgiveness. But kissing Eliza? Savor. Commit this to memory.

None of his previous affairs equaled the intensity of what he'd shared here with her. They didn't even have actual sex yet, and it had already moved beyond all familiarity—and intimacy, for he'd never discussed his innermost thoughts and emotions with another woman before.

As soon as he clasped her breast, the sound of a horse's harness filled his hearing.

Of all nights.

Reluctantly, he broke the kiss. "Gather the bedding, then head for the guest room and hide. Quickly now."

Tremain struggled to his feet and dressed swiftly, leaving the shirt open. He grabbed one of the blankets and tossed it onto the couch as she ran from the room. Smart girl, she took her cloak as well.

Grasping his cane, he hobbled to the door and opened it.

William Treacher removed his hat. "Beggin' yer pardon, Mr. Colson. My younger brother, Jacob, requires yer presence. His wife, God bless her, had a difficult birth. The baby—well, the wee lad didn't make it, and it seems Hannah won't either, so the doctor says. Jacob would like ye to say the prayers over them."

"Of course, come in. I fell asleep in front of the fire."

William wiped his feet and stepped across the threshold. "Aye, explains why yer all flushed."

Tremain nearly laughed aloud.

That is not quite the reason.

His entire body cried out for more of Eliza. Not tonight, it would seem.

In Tremain's more than two years of serving the village and surrounding area, he'd said prayers over two women who'd died in childbirth. This call would make number three. It never got any easier.

"Take a seat, William. I'll be out directly."

"I'll take ye in my wagon, Vicar. It'll save time."

After leaving his cane by the chair, Tremain hobbled down the hall, changed his shirt, attached his collar, and pulled on his coat. He grabbed his copy of the *Common Book of Prayer* and stepped into the guestroom. "Eliza," he whispered.

She stepped out of the shadow. "Yes."

Looping his free arm around her waist, he pulled her close, and he was already becoming aroused again. "Come tomorrow night. Same time. Will you?"

"Yes."

He kissed her hard, then stepped back. "Wait at least ten minutes before you leave. Don't bother locking the door."

"I heard. Not a pleasant way for the evening to end," she said sadly.

"No. Duty calls."

He closed the door behind him and slowly made his way to the parlor. After slipping on his greatcoat, he reached for the cane and followed William outside.

Yes, duty called.

And despite the sad circumstances, Tremain did not dread it for once.

Chapter 17

IF THERE EVER WAS A time Tremain was glad of his war experiences, it was tonight, for it steeled him for sickroom. The smell of rot and blood slammed his senses as soon as he crossed the Treacher's modest farmhouse threshold. Although the odors of a battlefield were familiar to him, his stomach churned here all the same. William escorted him to the primary bedroom. Hannah Treacher lay with a blanket tucked under her chin.

The only other person in the room was Dr. Edwards, wiping his bloody hands on a towel. "She passed about ten minutes ago, Vicar."

"What happened?"

"The family called me in two hours ago. A midwife handled the birth. Poor Mrs. Treacher remained in labor all day. A great loss of blood. Mind where you step."

Tremain recoiled at the pools of blood collected on the bed and floor. Bloody towels and cloths lay in a heap.

"Sepsis and gas gangrene, there was no stopping the infection," the doctor continued. "The poor woman began to rot before she passed. That's the smell. The baby didn't survive the trauma of his birth." Dr. Edwards tossed the bloody cloth to the pile. "Even if I were called in sooner, I could have done nothing. Not the midwife's fault. Just one of those things."

One of those things.

"Where is Jacob?" Tremain asked.

"The family is with him in the kitchen. He said he hopes you understand, but he cannot return to this room."

After glancing about the darkened space, Tremain agreed. This room *was* a battlefield where women had fought to save a young mother and her baby. Without warning, he grew dizzy; the indistinct sounds of rifle shots and cries of anguish filled his hearing. Ghostly arms pulled him into his war terrors while he was conscious.

No. I will not let this happen.

Bad enough that they haunted his nights, the horrors would *not* affect his life while awake. Closing his eyes tight, he willed back the images, smells, and sounds.

You will not claim me, not this day.

The images dissipated, and with an exhale, he stepped closer, the smell almost too much to bear. Next to Hannah on the bed was a small wrapped bundle. No doubt the newborn. Life could be brutal. And so could death.

"Father of all, we pray to you for Hannah Treacher and her baby...." He glanced at the doctor, who mouthed, 'Jacob.' "Jacob Treacher, and for all those whom we love but see no longer. Grant to them eternal rest. May Hannah and Jacob's souls and the souls of all the departed, through the mercy of God, rest in peace. Amen."

The two men left the room, closing the door behind them. Dr. Edwards whispered, "It's obvious the family will have to forgo the wake. They must be buried immediately."

"I concur, Dr. Edwards. I'll ensure they are laid to rest before noon."

The doctor placed his hat on his head, his other hand clasping his leather satchel. "A bad business. Tragic. Hannah's first birthing was smooth sailing. But this—everything that could go wrong—did. Out of my hands and into yours and God's, I imagine. I bid you goodnight, Vicar."

Dr. Edwards sounded weary, and Tremain couldn't blame him. "Goodnight, Doctor."

Tremain made his way to the kitchen. A cluster of people stood around the outer edges of the room. Sitting at the table were William, Jacob—now a widower—and curled up asleep in his lap, a little girl of about three years of age.

Jacob was twenty-eight, a tall, good-looking man who had chosen for a bride a kind and sturdy young woman he had grown up with. Tremain often observed the couple at Sunday services, and their love and respect for each other were evident.

A tragedy indeed.

Since Jacob was handsome and honorable, Tremain doubted he would remain a widower for long. Eventually, if and when the grief lessened, he would need a helpmate and a mother for the girl. A companion for his life and, if blessed, for his heart. Far from the strictures of London society, most common folk did not have the luxury of observing stringent periods of mourning. Unfortunately, life marched on and held many demands and responsibilities.

Jacob glanced up at him, his clear blue eyes moist and beseeching. Tremain laid a comforting hand on the man's shoulder.

In a low voice, Tremain said, "Everyone, gather around." The family shuffled closer. "Hannah and young Jacob are gone from this earthly dwelling, leaving behind those who mourn their absence. Grant that we may hold their memory dear, never bitter for what we have lost nor in regret for the past, but always in the hope of the eternal Kingdom where you will bring us together again. Through Christ our Lord."

The family murmured 'amen' in reply. Jacob's mother gathered the sleeping girl and took her from the room.

Tears fell freely from Jacob. "She's in a better place, her and the wee one, aren't they, Vicar? They've gone to a better place."

In this circumstance, speaking *his* truth would not suffice. Not to a young man mourning his wife and child. A man mired in deep grief and misery.

Tremain squeezed the farmer's shoulder. "Yes. They've gone to a better place. Their troubles are behind them, and their suffering is at an end. They're both at peace, Jacob. Take comfort in that."

He nodded. "S-s-she...Hannah told me to find love again, to be happy. She made me promise—" his voice broke.

"Then you must do as she asked. Mourn her, never forget her, but remember to live and love. Let light and hope into your heart."

Jacob turned and buried his head between his arms on the table, his broad shoulders shaking as he sobbed openly. Jacob's mother, who had returned to the room moments before, rushed to her son's side, rubbing his back in comfort.

Tremain quietly left the room. There was no more he could do for the anguished farmer tonight. Finding William and Mr. Treacher, he relayed the doctor's instructions for a swift burial. Tremain offered to stop by the gravediggers' houses on the way back to the vicarage. As William escorted him to the wagon, the words Tremain had spoken to Jacob reverberated in his mind.

"Remember to live and love. Let light and hope into your heart."

The time had come for him to follow the sage advice.

ELIZA HEARD OF THE tragic death of Mrs. Treacher from the servants at breakfast, and while she sympathized with the young farmer and his family, her heart also ached for Tremain. Gossip usually spared no details, and neither had this conversation, which was particularly gruesome considering they were all eating breakfast. Giving birth could be dangerous indeed.

Tremain had witnessed death as a soldier and as a vicar. In whatever circumstance, it must be brutal to see regardless. While nibbling on her scone, she wondered if she would have the inner strength to stand by his side as his wife.

Me? Married to a member of the clergy?

Why was she entertaining such a possibility? But Eliza often had of late. Indulging in daydreams had fallen by the wayside when she left school. Reality had tamped them down good and proper. Not even with William did she allow them to surface. That she readily entered into physical relations with the only two men she'd been in close proximity with gave her pause.

Though she'd rushed into her brief affair with William Winters more out of loneliness than deep affection, those reasons did not factor into her relationship with Tremain. Her feelings for Tremain were vastly different. All it took was for him to walk into a room, and her heart raced. Seeing him struggle to hide his emotions behind his stony mask touched her deeply. The man needed to heal, and she wanted to help him however she could.

Sighing, Eliza buttered the other half of her scone as the conversation around her faded. It would be a lot to take on. What would a vicar's wife do, exactly? Why not a governess and a vicar? They would be a good match intellectually. They would be a perfect match in bed if last night were any indication. She could put up with almost anything for a truly loving and passionate partnership —even being a vicar's wife. She'd attend services as long as she could stare at him. Accompany him on visits, smile, and drink tea, knowing at night and in bed; he would be hers and hers alone.

"Miss Winston?"

Eliza started, pulled from her girlish fantasies. "Sorry, I didn't hear what you said."

"Mr. Dibley will attend the funeral at noon to represent the viscount. Should any of us go?" Anna asked.

"Did you know Mrs. Treacher?"

Anna smiled. "Aye. More when we were girls. The village was abuzz when she caught Jacob Treacher. You couldn't find a finer-looking man in the area. Well, except for maybe the vicar. Though he be a cripple."

"Here now, none of that. Don't use that word," Mrs. Hughes, the cook, admonished. "The vicar gets around well enough."

"I meant nothing by it. Just saying it's a fact. Doesn't stop me from admiring Mr. Colson," Anna replied.

"Give over, you moony gel," Mrs. Hughes laughed. "As if the vicar would look your way. Clear the table now, and sharpish."

Anna shrugged and reached for the empty plates. "I don't want the man; he be too stiff and cold for me. All I'm saying is the vicar's pleasing to the eye."

Eliza agreed with Anna on that point, but she was dead wrong on the stiff and cold part. "Since you knew Mrs. Treacher, perhaps you should go with Mr. Dibley to the funeral."

Anna blushed. Ah. The maid harbored a *tendre* for the land steward. She couldn't blame her. He was an attractive man. Why not? A little above the maid's station, but no more than a vicar was above a governess. Eliza firmly believed that people from vastly different social classes would *never* be able to make a go of it. Too many obstacles. Too much heartache. How fortunate she and Tremain didn't have to be concerned about such a scenario. Should things come to that.

Popping the last of her scone into her mouth, she stood. "I'll let Mr. Dibley know you'll accompany him."

Anna blushed once again. "Thank you, Miss Winston."

Making her way upstairs, Eliza thought of tonight's rendezvous. As frightening as the prospect seemed, she would lay her feelings bare to Tremain and let events unfold as they may. One day at a time, he had said.

Prudent advice.

Chapter 18

A HELLISH DAY.

Funerals always depressed him utterly. Tremain sat by the fire with a glass of scotch tightly clutched in his hand. Between glancing at the clock and awaiting Eliza's arrival, he sipped his drink, wondering if inviting her here had been a wise plan. Fingering the various correspondence on his desk, including a couple he had picked up yesterday in the village, he dug through the pile to find another letter from Spencer. Shame covered him for not replying to the first one.

Pushing his drink aside, he slipped on his spectacles, slid the opener under the flap, and removed the letter. As was typical of Spence, brief and to the point. No pleasantries or wasted information.

I've already written to Mother and Father and also to Harry. The news? Phil and I are to be married. It will take place the third week of May at Gransford Manor (Mother and Father insisted, and I could hardly refuse, as you can well imagine). It will be a private affair. Family only. I want you here as my best man.

And you are. The best man and friend a brother could have. Harry will walk Phil down the aisle, and Mother plans a small but lavish breakfast.

Let me know how you are and if you will be attending. Please say yes.

Spence

Tremain took the pen, dipped it in ink, and began to write on a blank piece of paper.

DEAR SPENCE,

First, forgive me for my tardiness in replying. I have no excuse but to say duty has kept me busy. I also wanted time to digest your reply to my rather self-pitying letter from December. I've been wallowing far too much of late in a pool of guilt and other indulgent selfishness.

Going forward, I will endeavor to heal and live as you advise. I've already taken the first steps. A young woman here has me re-assessing many things. More on that later. Best to see if it leads anywhere first.

But more importantly, I was so delighted to hear of your news. I would be humbled and honored to stand up with you at your marriage ceremony. I will clear my schedule to ensure I am there for the entire week. It is time for me to climb out of this pit. And embrace life. And family. I cannot wait to see you all and meet Philomena.

Love,

Tremain

PULLING OUT A FRESH piece of paper, he wrote something similar to his parents, apologizing for his self-isolation and not responding sooner. He left out the part about Eliza for now but informed them he would be at Gransford Manor in May. It would be their first time together in over two years.

When he completed that letter, he started another. This one was to his older brother, Harrison. He had yet to learn what Harry was up to lately, as the letter writing had ceased on both sides. Apologies, recriminations, and heartfelt emotions poured out of him and onto the page with all his family letters. Regardless of his initial motivations in hiding himself away, at the core, he'd been egotistic in his response, to a point. Part of it *was* altruistic. He wanted to serve. But Tremain slowly realized that closing off one's heart is not the way to go about it.

Sitting back, Tremain rubbed his hand as it was cramping from all the writing. When the spasms relented, he picked up the glass and took a sip, reveling in the burn. His thoughts turned to Eliza.

Best to see if it leads anywhere first.

Really? Was he honestly considering it? Was he ready to engage in a relationship with her? He would turn her away if he possessed any honor and not indulge in any physical pleasure until he'd told her everything. Not only that, but the brief horror of being pulled into his war terror during his waking hours was making him re-examine a future with *any* woman.

Considering this, perhaps he should turn her away tonight. It would no doubt exhaust her patience with him. How any woman could endure his coldness, lay beyond his comprehension.

From the beginning, Eliza saw past the emotional part of his disguise.

Last night's activities had been a revelation. At first, he thought the heightened emotions stemmed from the fact he'd not been with a woman in more than three years. But ruminating over his past affair with Lady Trimly, he concluded the time spent with his mistress had left him empty.

During their affair, he indulged her fantasies in all ways, with bondage and domination on both sides. He never had such a bold and unscrupulous lover before. The flame of desire blew out quickly on his end. When her ladyship suggested inviting other people into the bedroom, he decided to end it, as he had reached his maximum level of licentiousness. Luckily the war intervened, and he took the opportunity to end things between them, claiming it was unfair of her to wait for his return. In truth, he was relieved to be rid of her, like scrubbing off a particularly dirty layer of grime from his skin.

At thirty-one years of age, he no longer desired fleeting, empty affairs. Tremain could no longer deny his feelings for Eliza nor push her away. If Spence could embrace love, undoubtedly, he could as well.

Disclosure. Honesty. No more doubts.

He should confess that he was Viscount Hawkestone, the son of the Duke of Gransford and not only a modest country vicar. But the conversation was not one he was capable of having this night. Tomorrow will bring clarity and courage. What utter bollocks. The sooner he told her, the better. It should be tonight. It *must* be tonight.

A soft knock sounded at the door. After placing the letters on the table, Tremain clasped his cane and hobbled to the door. Upon opening it, the rush of emotions that flooded him at seeing Eliza nearly buckled his knees. The cane clattered to the floor as he pulled her into an embrace. Her softness and warmth immediately soothed and aroused him. All his intentions of speaking the truth flew right out the window.

She hugged him back, rubbing against him and uttering a husky moan. "We might be seen."

"I no longer care," Tremain whispered hoarsely. He gave her a devastating kiss filled with urgency to prove the point. He stepped back, bringing her with him, not breaking the connection, and kicked the door shut with his boot.

He broke the kiss and divested her of her cloak, letting it fall to the floor. She wore a floral frock that hugged her luscious curves.

"I am wearing nothing under this modest gown."

Groaning in response to her sensual confession, Tremain kissed her again, cupping her face to hold her still while he ravished her mouth. For having little experience, Eliza was confident in her sexuality, which made her all the more appealing. He was under her spell, in complete thrall to her.

Clasping her arm gently, he pulled her toward his room, limping but staying on his feet. Once inside, he kissed her again, more fervently than before, if possible. His mind swirled, and all rational thought left him, along with the urgent need for honest conversation.

"I need to see you naked," Tremain growled huskily.

Eliza reached into the side pocket of her gown and held out a small tin. "Sheaths." She flushed, clearly embarrassed.

Tremain took the tin and placed it on the bedside table. Turning back to face her, he smiled. "My sweet, no need to be nervous. You had an affair with a man in the past, and you should not feel ashamed. I could nearly fill this room with my past lovers. It's in *my* past. I've made many mistakes in my life. We try and learn from them and move forward. It's something I am still grappling with."

"Me as well."

"The earl's son means nothing to you. Correct?"

Eliza cupped his cheek. "No. Nothing. But you, Trey, mean everything."

The fact that she used his nickname made his heart clench. "As do you. Let us banish past experiences. I did not intend to brag about my previous dalliances filling the room. As you can see, this room is not all that large." Eliza smiled in response. "I merely wished to convey that none of them touched my heart as you do. Tonight is about us—and no one else. Agreed?"

Eliza nodded as she unbuttoned her gown. It pooled at her feet, leaving her gloriously naked. Her alabaster skin gleamed from the firelight and the subdued illumination from the nearby gas lamp. Abundant curves, full breasts, and long, coltish legs stirred his desire to unknown heights. Freckles dotted various parts of her lush body, and he vowed to become acquainted with every one of them.

"You are stunning. Utterly beautiful," Tremain murmured with awe.

"Let me see all of you. Take off your clothes," Eliza whispered.

Tremain pulled his shirt over his head and threw it to the floor. Toeing off his shoes, he kicked them aside. He didn't wear hose or undergarments tonight. She watched him, her heated gaze riveted on him, slowly unbuttoning his trousers. A twinge of self-consciousness flooded him concerning his injury and how it may affect his performance. His slight hesitation caused her to assist him in pulling down his trousers. His erection sprang free.

"You are magnificent. In all ways." Eliza gripped him, causing him to groan. She stroked his cock as she explored his chest, her tongue licking one of his nipples. "I want you to do wild and wicked things to me. Things I don't quite understand but long for nonetheless."

No doubt of it, Tremain could happily die here and now. Tumbling onto his large bed, they reached for each other, kissing and touching, naked skin to naked skin. He kissed her neck, then trailed his lips to an erect nipple. Clamping his mouth over it, his hand moved between her legs, stroking in tandem with his sucking.

My dear, wild Eliza.

Finding the nub of sensitive nerves, he rubbed it and suckled her breast until she moaned and writhed. Tremain plunged two fingers inside her, causing her to cry out.

Ah. So wet.

So ready for him.

"Yes!" she cried.

He increased the pace until her moans grew louder. The air in the room thrummed with desire. They panted and groaned, covered in a thin sheen of sweat from their excursions. He was so hard, completely lost in a sensual haze. Seeing to her pleasure was his only thought, his only goal.

Eliza cried out, shaking with her release. He lay flat, bringing her in close, her head resting on his chest.

"That was wonderful," Eliza sighed.

"And yet, there is more to come. Do you wish us to go further?" He kissed her forehead, smoothing aside her hair.

Please say yes, I beg of you.

"Yes."

Relief covered him. Gently clasping Eliza's arm, Tremain pulled her on top of him.

"My weight will be pressing against your thigh," she said, clearly concerned.

"Let's try. Grab a sheath and put it on me."

Eliza did, and when her fingers gripped his cock, he moaned. He was ready to come apart already; it wouldn't take much. It had been so long since he'd been with a woman. But this was more than mere sex for gratification's sake.

It meant the world. Eliza meant—the world entire.

"I've never done it this way," she murmured. "In this position."

"Then you're in for a treat. It's one of my favorites," Tremain teased.

Rising, she grasped him tighter while slowly descending his length. Tremain slid in deeper and moaned at the tightness that greeted him.

"My," Eliza marveled. "How you fill me." She straddled his thighs, and a white-hot stab of pain ran down his right leg, causing him to groan.

She stilled. "Did I hurt you?"

Damn.

After taking a cleansing breath and exhaling, he said, "Lean forward a bit, rest your hands on my shoulders—that's it. Not as much pressure on my thigh. The pain has lessened already. Now, move, Eliza. Ride me. Take your pleasure. Make love to me."

"Yes. Make love." Eliza found a steady pace, and her hardened nub rubbed against his sheathed cock. Eliza threw back her head, her golden waves cascading down her back. Gripping both breasts, she pushed them together while fingering her nipples. The erotic sight drove him insane, causing him to forget all lingering pain. Gripping her hips, he drove up inside of her, thrusting hard.

"Do it again, I beg you. Touch your breasts, play with them." Tremain's voice was husky and pleading.

Never begged before—another first.

Being with Eliza heightened his emotions, filling his heart to bursting.

Eliza did as he pleaded, the apparent sensual euphoria clear on her beautiful face. She moaned, clearly enjoying the pleasure she gave herself—and him.

Their movements grew more frantic, their breathing rough and wild.

"Let me suck it," he growled. "Give me your breast."

Eliza leaned in, kissing his cheek as he latched onto her nipple. The overwhelming desire caused his head to swim.

The feel of her, the scent of her soft skin.

It had ignited him from the inside out, like a runaway blaze in a dry forest. There was no holding back. Tremain didn't even try. A powerful climax slammed him hard, his body shaking with his forceful release.

Every tendon in his body tightened, causing his legs to go rigid. For a brief moment, he experienced no pain, only earth-shattering bliss. Eliza grasped the headboard and moved faster, rocking, moaning, lost in her enjoyment. Then she cried out, her inner muscles clutching him as wave after wave of ecstasy hit her. With a ragged cry, she collapsed, laying her head against his chest. They stayed joined, quietly waiting for their breathing to return to normal.

"Trey...my God."

With all restraints removed, they had reveled in their wild passion. Caressing Eliza's arm, he realized that it wasn't enough.

He wanted more. He wanted it *all*.

But as calm settled over him, the pain returned, so he gently urged Eliza to lay by his side.

With a grunt, he stood and reached for the rubbish bin. Removing the sheath, he tossed it in. Glancing at Eliza, he smiled. She looked gloriously disheveled, holding the blanket to her chin, her hair spilling about her shoulders. Her face was flushed, her lips red from his aggressive kisses.

Something hitched and moved in Tremain's chest. He felt more alive than he had for years.

Perhaps ever.

After they rested, he wanted to go again.

All night.

Chapter 19

ELIZA'S EXPERIENCE with William did not even come close to this depth of passion. The intimacy of what she and Tremain had shared made her breath hitch.

"Are you in pain?" she asked, worried. She had bounced up and down on top of him quite violently.

"A little. It's receding now."

"Was today horrible? The funeral, I mean? And last night? Unless you would rather not discuss it, I understand." Not precisely proper conversation after making love. But Eliza wanted to move the intimacy beyond the physical. To have him confide in her, share his day.

Tremain pulled her close so her head rested against his shoulder. "I've never seen childbirth go so wrong. Enough to frighten any man from getting his wife with child, I assure you."

"I heard some of the stories from the servants. How dreadfully sad for Mr. Treacher and his daughter," she said softly.

"The gravediggers arrived at first light, and we had the poor woman and her infant in the ground before noon. Tragic indeed. I said prayers and offered sympathy and condolence, but ultimately, I don't believe I helped much."

Eliza leaned up on her elbow. "That's not true. I heard you were a great comfort to the poor man."

"How did you hear that?"

"From Anna. She attended the service with Mr. Dibley. She observed how you comforted the family, and Mrs. Treacher's sister declared you were a strong and steady presence the night before."

Tremain scoffed. "Strong and steady? Hardly. I walked into that bedroom and became paralyzed with fear. It was the smell, you see. Rot, blood, and death. It took me back to the Transvaal. That's never happened before in my cognizant state. It terrifies me." He let out a ragged breath and continued. "Perhaps it was a warning or an omen if I believed in such things, telling me I will never be whole."

Eliza sat upright and shook her head. "No. I don't accept that. How long did the episode last?"

"Not long. I willed it away."

"There, you see? You didn't allow the fear to overtake you. You fought it. You've been through a horrific ordeal due to the war. It will take time to mend." She kissed his cheek. "I'm glad you shared this with me and told me about your nightmares. Sharing burdens with others is the only way you can move past it. And you will. You're a strong, compassionate man."

Tremain gazed up at her. "Am I? Well, if you believe it, then so shall I."

She curled up next to him again. "Believe it. And confide in those who care for you. In those who—love you. And I do, Trey. I love you."

Tremain didn't reply. Logs snapping and crackling in the hearth were the only sound in the room.

Heavens, she didn't mean for those words to slip out. Leave it to her to muck things up and—Tremain pulled her on top of him and gave her a heated kiss. He slipped his tongue inside her mouth and tasted her. His erection pressed insistently against her abdomen.

"You love me?" he whispered as he laid hot kisses along her chin to her ear. "Truly love me? This broken, frozen shell of a man?"

"Yes, although you annoy me beyond all endurance with your shifting and unpredictable emotions, I love you all the more for it. Explain that."

Tremain pulled her close, rolled over, and looked down at her. "For the life of me, I cannot explain it. But I embrace it wholeheartedly. You're a brave and beautiful woman, and I absolutely adore you." He leaned in and whispered, "And I love you with what remains of my heart. For you are making it whole again."

A surge of happiness tore through Eliza making her heart thump madly. They kissed long and deep. They stopped kissing only long enough to fit him with another sheath. When Tremain thrust into her with a slick glide, her back arched, and she cried out from the sheer joy of him inside her—loving her.

Wrapping her legs and arms around him, she met every push and slide of his shaft and angled her hips upward, further stimulating her sensitive nub. They rocked in each other's arms, moaning, kissing, and touching. Tremain laced his fingers through hers, raising their joined hands to lay flat beside her head. With a slow, steady, and thoroughly excellent rhythm, he loved her. Deep. Eliza had no idea how much time passed, nor did she care. He took deliberate care, kissing, caressing, leaving no part of her untouched.

The pace quickened, bringing them both to unknown heights.

"This is love," Tremain rumbled, awe in his voice.

With a ragged gasp, she climaxed, and Tremain was there with her at nearly the same instant. Grimacing, he rolled off her. With teeth clenched, he fisted the bedding. Glancing down at his right leg, she could see the damaged muscles were pulled taut, the limb rigid and unyielding.

"Cramps...Christ, the pain." His voice was strained and hoarse.

Eliza scrambled out of bed and quickly dressed. "It will only take me a few moments to do up another mustard plaster."

"Bring the whiskey. It's in the parlor," Tremain groaned.

Running down the hall, Eliza wondered if it would always be like this. Would they only be able to enjoy sex at the expense of his pain? Regardless, she would assist him and do whatever it took to bring him relief, either physically or emotionally.

It would not be easy loving Tremain Colson, but she would embrace it nonetheless.

THE FIRST JOLT OF UNBEARABLE pain hit him right after he started thrusting, but for the life of him, he could not pull away from her sweet softness regardless of the anguish he'd suffered. Evidently, he would have to forego that particular position in the future.

If they *had* a future

Admitting their feelings was one thing, but there was much more to reveal and consider. The insistent throbbing had scrambled Tremain's brain, and, as a result, he couldn't discuss the particular subject of his identity and all that entailed. Not tonight.

Eliza loved him.

The declaration shocked as well as honored him. Eliza's affirmation sorted his feelings—feelings he'd denied for weeks.

Throwing his arm over his eyes, he tried to focus on anything but the pain. But he couldn't. What a bloody mess he was in. Jon had warned him that his duplicity could cause any number of problems. But Tremain hadn't counted on falling in love.

Eliza entered the room. "Lay on your side," she instructed.

He did and exhaled with relief when the plaster made contact with the hammering ache in his thigh and leg. Eliza hurried from the room, returning with the decanter. She poured him a generous glass. After he took a large gulp, he hissed through his teeth as the single malt burned a fiery trail down his throat.

Sweet, blessed respite.

"Any relief?"

"Some. Thank you. You must think me weak in body as well as mind. It hasn't been easy. I often feel like I'm standing on the edge of a precipice. When someone hovers near such hopelessness, it is easy to take that final step and end it. I know of a couple of my fellow soldiers who did exactly that. I don't condemn them nor think them pathetic." Tremain took another sip of scotch. "The choice was before me. I wanted to live. To heal. So I entered the church."

Good God, I'm babbling. It seems as if I am discussing this—to a point.

"To give back to your fellow man, as you said."

"Yes."

"I cannot begin to imagine all you've gone through, nor do I think you weak of mind or body. But I wish to do what I can—to support you. That's what people in love do for each other, I believe. Will you tell me of your nightmare?"

Could he?

Tremain didn't go into any great detail, nor did he reveal his status as a captain, which would raise questions he did not want to answer tonight. He even skimmed over the gorier details of the Battle of Rorke's Drift, but by the way Eliza's eyes widened as he spoke, he had told her enough to capture the horror of that day.

"What happened after the men carried you out of the hospital?" she asked breathlessly.

"I was propped up by the storehouse, utterly useless for battle, but during my more lucid moments, I assisted in handing out ammunition to nearby soldiers. The battle lasted all through the night. Dead bodies lay all around me, yet I managed to survive. Only when Chelmsford's column could be seen approaching from Isandlwana, the Zulus turned and left." He snorted. "Because of my injury, I was not at Isandlwana for the brutal slaughter of my fellow soldiers and friends. I carry that guilt. So many killed."

"But you were not. Thank God."

"Not certain why I was spared, but I felt honor bound to serve in a way that did not involve killing and war. I've had my fill of soldiering."

Eliza dashed a tear away from her cheek. "Thank you for telling me."

"Can you imagine? The generals placed me on a list with the rest of the lads from the hospital for a Victoria Cross. I had intended to refuse it, but Sir Garnet Wolseley removed my name. He claimed it was monstrous making heroes out of those shut up in a building fighting like rats. Regardless, the others eventually received it and deservedly so." Tremain did not reveal that he and Wolseley despised each other dating back to when he served under him during the Anglo-Ashanti War in 1874. It was the reason Tremain eventually transferred to the 24th Regiment of Foot.

Eliza began to massage his leg, so he closed his eyes and relaxed, allowing the heat from the plaster and her intoxicating touch to dull the severe ache not only in his limb but in his soul. He'd never told anyone about Rorke's Drift. Not Jon, nor anyone in his family. And the confession—as it were—lifted a part of his burden of guilt and remorse.

Love was a powerful tool.

"You have yet to tell me anything of your family and past," Eliza said.

"I will. Very soon, I promise. It took all I had to reveal this much to you." He gave her a shaky smile. Tremain spoke the truth.

He couldn't divulge any more tonight. Exhaustion covered him. Blurting it out now would be a mistake, for he'd already made one tonight. Tremain never should have made love to her or declared his love without telling her his true identity. Yet another regret to add to his long list.

Eliza removed the plasters and tossed them in the nearby basin. "Understandable. Then I shall tell you a little about me. I was a headstrong girl who spoke my mind. I infuriated the nuns to no end."

He chuckled. "I can well imagine."

"I made many friends there, but we've all lost contact. We had quite a tight-knit group. We all made up stories of what we wished to happen with our lives. It consisted of the usual fantasies of a knight of old or a prince riding up on a magnificent steed to rescue us from poverty and drudgery." Her eyes twinkled at the memories.

And what of a disabled vicar riding in a rickety wagon?

The question lay on the tip of his tongue, but he decided against voicing it aloud. Yes, a vicar who is not what he seems. A vicar who is a coward as well as a liar.

Enough.

He pushed those disturbing thoughts away. Tremain caressed her cheek. "And did you dream of a knight or prince?"

A soft laugh escaped her. "Neither. I wanted a tall, burly Highlander or a rugged Viking. I dreamed of wild, long-haired warriors who clasped huge swords and wore furs. Men who would lay down their lives to protect me. See to my pleasure, but virile enough to handle my passion and not feel threatened by it. Truthfully, I've had many naughty thoughts from an early age, along with a vivid imagination. I still do."

"I am eternally grateful for it." He trailed the tips of his fingers across her sensual mouth.

Eliza grasped his hand and kissed his palm, then stood. "I should say goodnight. The hour grows late, and I should return in case the staff misses me."

Tremain frowned. He didn't want her to leave. Gazing at her standing in the firelight, Tremain reveled in how her garments hugged her abundant curves, which sparked his arousal anew. He held on to the bedpost, and, using it as leverage, he rose to his feet and turned to face her, naked and erect. "Are you sure you wish to leave at this exact moment?" he said, his voice low and husky.

Eliza smiled and stood before him. "Why should I stay?" she teased.

Snaking an arm about her waist, Tremain pulled her close and kissed her hard. She ran her hands through his hair, fisting it as they kissed and their tongues joined.

"Get a sheath, and I will show you why you should stay a few minutes more." So much for exhaustion. And so much for his guilt. There would be time enough to examine his actions in the cold light of day.

She retrieved an envelope from the tin, then rolled it onto his erect prick. With a swift motion, he turned her to face the bed, then spread his hand flat on her back, gently pushing her downward. Grabbing the hem of her skirt, he raised it.

"Trey—oh," she moaned.

Tremain had always enjoyed *this* position. So far, it did not place undue pressure on his leg and thigh.

Eliza's beauty caused his heart to hitch. He caressed the soft globes of her rear with trembling hands, then slipped one hand between her legs.

Wet. Such a passionate woman.

With no warning, he plunged into her. Eliza met each eager thrust, pushing back against him as he slipped in deeper. Wrapping her golden locks about his wrist, Tremain pulled gently. "Touch yourself, Eliza."

Her hand disappeared between her legs, and she rubbed her hardened nub while he continued his ceaseless pounding. They both cried out at nearly the same time. He stood upright when he caught his breath, slipping out of her. After lowering her skirt, Tremain assisted her in standing upright, then embraced her from behind. Eliza held his arms, and they swayed together, reveling in the closeness. An invisible but strong bond had formed between them tonight.

"Go," he whispered ardently in her ear. "Go now before I take you again. And again."

Eliza broke from him and ran for the door. Then she stopped, turned, and gave him a sultry smile before disappearing into the hall and out the front door.

Tremain sat on the edge of the bed, his body still shaking from the intensity of their joining.

He was lost.

Utterly besotted. Completely in love.

And he had the distinct feeling when he *did* reveal the rest of his story; he could very well lose her.

Chapter 20

ELIZA AWOKE ACHING and sore the following day but reveled in the sensation. Stretching like a lazy cat, she sighed contentedly, reliving her night with Tremain. The emotions were so overwhelming she thought her heart would burst.

How satisfying to find that Tremain proved to be every inch the passionate lover she knew he would be. Under the protective shield, she had found an intense and desirous heat. The sex went far beyond what she'd experienced with William. But then, with Tremain, love was happily in the mix.

She *loved* him.

It had built at a slow but steady pace. The more Tremain had revealed, the more she fell for him. For such a man, she could become a vicar's wife. But she was getting ahead of herself. There was no mention of anything relatively so permanent as marriage. It would bear consideration on both their parts. How tempting to run to the vicarage, throw herself into his strong embrace, and beg him to love her again.

He *loved* her.

Tremain had declared it.

Could she be any happier? Someone in this world *loved* her—cared for her. What a glorious feeling.

Enough romantic musings for now, as she had much to attend to today. Eliza sat upright and stretched once again. Yesterday, Drew had shyly revealed his birthday was this coming Sunday. A small party would be just the thing. She must speak to Mrs. Hughes and arrange a special meal, then make a trip to the village to order one of Mrs. Tompkins's chocolate cakes, as the lad adored it.

Once she performed her ablutions and dressed in one of her gray gowns, she hurried to the kitchen and ate toast and tea with the staff, informing them of Drew's upcoming tenth birthday.

Mrs. Hughes frowned, crossing her arms under her ample bosom. "And what is wrong with *my* cakes that you must hie off to the pub to get one?"

Eliza smiled. "Nothing whatsoever. It's Drew's favorite; you will have enough to do with the meal. I hear he enjoys seed cake; perhaps that and lemon tarts would be a nice accompaniment. Just a suggestion."

The cook nodded. "Aye, fair enough. I'll get word to the butcher to deliver a nice beef loin. How many will be attending?"

"Let's see. Mr. Dibley, the vicar, Mr. and Mrs. Tompkins, the rest of the staff, and myself."

"Here now. I've never ate in the dining room in my life. 'Tisn't done. 'Tisn't proper," Mrs. Hughes sniffed.

Eliza stood. "I'll run it by Mr. Dibley later this afternoon, but I already know what he will say: it's right and proper for *this* house." She gave the cook an affectionate smile. "The poor boy lost his mother. He has no other family and looks to all of us to fill that role. Drew said that we're the only friends he has."

Mrs. Hughes dabbed her eyes with the corner of her apron. "Poor wee mite. Aye, he's a darling lad. We'll be there, and I'll make all his favorites."

Eliza patted Mrs. Hughes's arm and headed upstairs to the schoolroom. If anyone understood what it felt like to be without a family or loved ones, Eliza did. She would make sure Drew was surrounded by love and support. Things she'd never truly experienced, but now with Tremain, they lay within her grasp.

LATER THAT AFTERNOON, Eliza assigned Drew two pages of math problems and told him they would go for a long walk if he finished before she returned. Now would be the perfect opportunity to head to the village and order the cake. Slipping on her cloak, she went in search of Jon Dibley. The study door was ajar, so Eliza knocked and stepped into the room, shocked to find Tremain sitting before the desk. Awareness skittered across her nerve endings at the sight of him. He looked handsome today, dressed all in black with his white collar. He and Mr. Dibley stood when she'd entered the room, though it took Tremain a little longer.

Tremain gave her a scorching gaze as if willing Eliza to recall every intense and intimate thing that had happened the night before. She flushed, her heart pounding at a fast pace. Mr. Dibley looked between them and raised an eyebrow but said nothing.

"Please sit, gentlemen. I'm on my way to the village to order a cake. Drew's birthday is this Sunday, and I'm arranging a small dinner celebration. I do hope you both can attend."

"I had no idea," Tremain said as he sat.

"He just revealed it to me. I thought to invite the Tompkinses and the rest of the staff unless you both object to dining with the servants. Mrs. Hughes responded, 'It isn't proper,' but I'm hoping we can overlook societal rules for the boy's sake for one night."

Mr. Dibley smiled. "I am one of the help, as it were, so I've no objections. Well, Vicar? Would it upset your sensibilities?"

Tremain cast Mr. Dibley a warning look, for what reason Eliza could not say. "Not at all. I would be happy to attend." He stood, leaning on his cane. "I'll accompany you to the village."

"Oh, there's no need. You both no doubt have business to discuss."

"We have finished for the day, correct, Mr. Dibley?"

Jon Dibley crossed his arms, looking highly amused. "It would seem so."

Tremain crooked his arm. "Shall we?"

Eliza slipped her arm through his, resting her hand on the sleeve of his frock coat. Muscle tensed under her fingers. As they stepped into the hall, he pulled her into a crushing embrace.

"God, how I've ached for you. I barely slept last night." Tremain kissed her, long and deep, igniting her passion afresh. "Come to me tonight. Say you will. I *need* you."

His demanding mouth found hers again, kissing her until she was breathless. Eliza broke the kiss and gazed up at him. The heat in his eyes caused her heart to hammer against her ribs. "I need you, too. Tonight. But for now, we must head for the village."

He grinned. His smile made him even more handsome. "Or we can go to my bed now and make love until the sun sets."

How tempting.

"Later, my passionate vicar," she teased.

"Yes, later. I also want us to talk. I have something to tell you."

"You can tell me now. We're alone."

"No, better it's tonight. What I have to say will take more time than we have here. It will not be a short conversation. Or an easy one."

He offered his arm again, and they walked outside into the early spring sunshine.

"You have me intrigued; can you not give me a hint?" she said.

"Best not."

"You *are* infuriating," she pouted.

"As you've already said."

The young coachman, Terrance, opened the carriage door and assisted them in. As soon as the door closed, Tremain pulled her into his lap and began to kiss her. His mouth demanded everything—and Eliza freely gave it.

Good thing the curtains were closed. Clasping Eliza's hand, Tremain tunneled under his coat until she felt the hardness pressing against the fall of his trousers. Encouraging her to clutch him tight, he kissed her again, more desperately than before. "What I would give to see you on your knees, my cock in your mouth. Am I being too blunt?"

Eliza gripped him tighter, and he groaned in response. "I would," she whispered, "But it's only a few minutes' journey."

"Lift your skirts, sit facing me, and rock back and forth. It won't take much to make me come."

She raised an eyebrow. "Won't it make a bit of a mess?"

"No one will know. I'll keep the coat buttoned while in the village. Quickly now."

She stood and lifted her gown and petticoats while he opened his coat. His erection strained against the fabric. Straddling him, she leaned forward to avoid putting pressure on his thigh.

"Yes. Perfect. Now move," Tremain commanded, his voice hard and rough.

She did, riding his stiff shaft for all it was worth. The scrap of linen from her drawers and the wool of his trousers were the only barriers between them. The swaying of the carriage enhanced their frenzied movements as it rumbled over the mud-packed path.

Eliza quickened the pace, kissing him deeply as she rubbed against his hardness. The excitement of trying to finish before they reached the village heightened her hunger and Tremain's, for he returned her kisses with equal enthusiasm.

Oh. Yes.

She buried her face in his shoulder to muffle her moans, as it took no time for her to reach her peak. Taking a cleansing breath, Eliza sat back and kept up the frantic pace. Tremain clenched his teeth as beads of perspiration broke out at his hairline as she rode him. Closing his eyes, he moaned, obviously reaching his climax. When they pulled up in front of The Rusty Cockerel, they sat opposite each other as if nothing happened.

"How do I look?" she murmured, straightening her gown.

"Like a woman well satisfied."

"Oh." Eliza touched her cheeks; they were hot and no doubt flushed. "Let's sit a moment before we go in."

The door opened. "Looks as if we must brave the public. You look pretty. Entirely respectable." His mouth quirked in amusement.

With a sigh of resignation, she stepped out with the assistance of the Tompkinses young lad. Tremain followed, his face showing an impassive mask of cool indifference. Drat the man for appearing calm and collected after their encounter. Eliza felt anything but.

After ordering the cake and inviting Mr. and Mrs. Tompkins to dinner Sunday evening, Tremain and Eliza walked to the corner shop, where she bought Drew some books.

"Are you getting him a gift?" she asked Tremain as they headed toward the carriage.

"I have it all in hand, do not worry. In fact, I—"

"Hawk! My God, is that you?" A shrill, feminine voice called out. Tremain froze, the muscles in his arm tightening under Eliza's fingers. "As I live and breathe, I cannot believe I would run into you in such an obscure hamlet such as this mud-hole."

The woman standing before them epitomized a wealthy English rose. Her exquisitely styled auburn hair, topped by a fashionable green taffeta bonnet, showed to advantage. The rest of her traveling outfit consisted of a silk gown in various shades of green and beige with lace at the collar and gold embroidery at the sleeves, all set off by a mink-trimmed wool cape. The beauty twirled a green parasol with her leather-gloved hands as she gave Tremain a sultry look that instantly sparked Eliza's jealousy.

Wait. What did the woman call him? Hawk?

"On your way to a vicars-and-tarts party? In this rustic country setting? Good to know your licentious nature is alive and well." The lady gave Tremain a teasing wink, and Eliza felt the ground shift beneath her.

"Though I daresay your companion is hardly dressed as a doxie," the lady continued as she gave Eliza a quick but indifferent appraisal. "Quite dowdy, if you don't mind me saying. Going to introduce us, Lord Hawkestone? Is this your latest paramour? If I knew you preferred a woman with golden hair, I would have dyed mine. But then, I always indulged you in matters of bed sport."

Eliza gasped in shock at the ribald talk and the name to which this woman referred to Tremain. This identification had to be a mistake. Her insides roiled; confusion filled her thoughts. Eliza glanced back and forth between them. Tremain looked thunderous. The woman looked smug and triumphant.

Lord Hawkestone.

It *cannot* be accurate.

Gasping in shock, Eliza clasped a hand over her mouth. Tremain was Viscount Hawkestone? The fragments all slid into place. His bearing, his accent, the expensive furnishings, and the icebox. His unwillingness to speak about his past. Everything that she thought she knew and believed in shattered into thousands of pieces.

Chapter 21

TREMAIN DID NOT HAVE to look at Eliza to know she was shocked. Anger would soon follow, and the hurt and this was not the place to hash it out. Blast it. He was going to tell her tonight. He even told her not an hour ago that they had to talk. Now it was too late—selfish fool.

He wouldn't allow the drama to play out in the middle of the village square. And be damned if he was introducing them. He clasped Eliza's arm, pulled her to the carriage, and opened the door. "Go home, Eliza, and return the carriage to me."

"Wait. This woman says you're Viscount Hawkestone?" Her voice was dull but filled with pain, tearing at his insides.

"Yes."

"Yes? That's it?" Her voice raised. Anger. There it was. He couldn't blame her. At *all*.

"I *will* explain everything. Just not here."

Eliza grasped the door and then slammed it shut. The carriage pulled away, leaving him to face his former lover.

Samantha bit her lower lip, no doubt to keep from laughing. "You have to admit this is all quite amusing."

Red fury covered him. He grabbed her elbow, pulling her toward the pub. They were already attracting attention in the street. Who knows what the village people overheard?

"Using your office for a moment, Mr. Tompkins." Tremain did not wait for a reply, merely thrust Lady Trimly into the room and slammed the door. "I see your manners have not improved, Samantha. I'll have you know Miss Winston is a respectable governess and did not warrant such shabby behavior."

Samantha laid her parasol on the desk and sat in the chair, meticulously arranging her gown. Then she lifted her head, studying him closely. A sharp bark of cynical laughter left her throat.

"Wait. Does Miss Winston think you're a vicar? *You?* Regardless, the woman did not look at you like a respectable governess but rather as a woman emotionally attached to you. One that knows you intimately. I found her open and frank adoration pathetic. The young miss was also shocked to hear of your title. Do not tell me you actually *are* a vicar?"

An even higher-pitched nasal laugh left her throat, causing him to cringe.

I always hated her grating giggles.

"Oh, this development is too juicy not to share," she continued, relishing this discovery. "Do you mean to say when your family told all and sundry you were off recovering from your war wounds on the Italian coast, you were here playing at being a saintly priest?" She laughed again, her head thrown back with delight. It would be tempting to wrap his hands about her delicate neck and squeeze—anything to shut her up.

"It's none of your damned business what I've been doing or what I am now," he snarled.

Samantha stopped laughing. "It is when I send you letters and receive no response. Did you get them? I sent them to your family's estate."

"I received them. I tossed them into the fire unopened."

Her eyes narrowed; her mouth turned down at the corners. "We are lovers, and it is common courtesy to answer my queries. I will not be disregarded."

Tremain leaned on his cane, his leg and thigh burning with agony enough to match his anger. "I severed the connection before leaving for South Africa, and you know it. There's nothing between us, nor am I interested in rekindling what little did exist. I'd rather chalk up the debauched affair to a brief moment of insanity. Your uncouth and unladylike behavior further serves to remind me why I ended the dalliance."

"How dare you speak to me this way?" she screamed. Her high-pitched voice was enough to shatter glass. "You're lucky I was willing to give you another chance, but now that I see that you're a cripple and a dour priest besides, be damned if I will." Samantha stood and moved toward the door, but Tremain caught her wrist to halt her exit.

"You decided to give me another chance when you learned I had become Viscount Hawkestone. No other reason," he snapped. "Don't pretend otherwise. I know of your ambition and rapacity."

"I don't deny it. If your older brother never marries, you will be the heir to the dukedom. It was a gamble worth taking."

God, what devious machinations.

Leave it to Lady Samantha Trimly to form such a cold-blooded scheme. "You will not repeat what you've seen here. Or that you saw me at all." Tremain squeezed her arm, and she winced but also flashed him a furious look of pure hatred. Hard to believe he'd once shared a bed with this woman.

Samantha stepped closer and glared up at him. "When you get down on your knees to pray, if you are even physically capable of doing so, do you ask forgiveness for your many and varied sins?" She smiled cruelly. "Is it like when you got down on your knees before me? Your mouth was occupied with other things besides prayers, if memory serves. Remember all the ways you tied me to the bed and fucked me? Or perhaps the time you made me get on my hands and knees and you—"

He stepped forward, grabbing her by the throat with his left hand. She sputtered foal oaths between each gasp of breath. With a grunt of disgust, he pulled his hand away. Keeping it there would only inflame her twisted lust. He understood that much about her.

Maintain control.

Briefly closing his eyes, he forcibly banked his rage. He would not give this woman what she wanted. "I'm not the same man who indulged your depraved fantasies. It's best you leave here as soon as possible," Tremain glowered, pointing to the door with his still raised hand.

Samantha's eyes gleamed with a mixture of malice and desire as she swept her hand under his coat and past his crotch, cupping his flaccid cock. "No. You're not the same man at all. A war injury?"

"No. I don't want you."

With a huff, she picked up her parasol and headed for the door. She turned to meet Tremain's gaze. "I'm on my way to London. The season is about to be in full swing, and I will ensure all are made aware of what I've observed here. How pitiable, the son of the Duke of Gransford, the virile Viscount Hawkestone, has lost his wits and is now a crippled, impotent country parson. A pathetic shell of his former self and an embarrassment to his family."

This was not how he wanted his stint as a clergyman to end. Now he would embarrass his family and subject them to scandalous gossip. Even when he tried to help people, they wound up hurt.

And Eliza? He'd seen the look in her eye, anger mixed with shock and disappointment. Tonight, he'd planned to tell her about his life and family and why he perpetuated his deception. Last night, Tremain had laid the groundwork when speaking of his war experiences. Damn it all; why didn't he tell her everything then and there? A major miscalculation.

Tremain walked over to the door and opened it. "Then you best be on your way to London." He had no idea why Samantha was in Hawksgreen, nor did he care.

With her chin raised in the air, Samantha swept from the room, leaving a cloying scent of heavy perfume in her wake. What possessed him to become involved with such a malicious, debauched creature?

Wearily, Tremain sank into the chair to wait for the carriage to return.

AT FIRST, TREMAIN WONDERED if Eliza would even bother to send the carriage back, but close to thirty minutes later, it pulled up in front of the pub.

"Home, Vicar?" Terrance asked.

Tremain stepped up into the coach. "No. Hawkestone Estate."

He sat back and frowned. If there was one thing he loathed, it was drama. He'd had his fill today. Perhaps it would be prudent to go to the vicarage instead, but he must see Eliza and try to explain. As pure as his motives were when he began this ruse more than two years ago, he fully acknowledged the selfishness behind the subterfuge. When one is the second son of a duke and brought up in an opulent setting, concern for others and their feelings often do not factor in decision-making. That was all on him.

Nonetheless, Tremain truly wanted to give something back. Under his devoutness and supposed self-sacrifice, Tremain also wished for forgiveness and healing of his battered soul. But at the crux of it all, he'd only thought of himself as he had the entirety of his life without thinking of how his actions would affect others.

His family. His friends. A small boy. The woman he loved.

Tremain leaped from the coach before it had stopped, dismissing the pain tearing up his leg. He banged on the front door with his walking stick and pushed through as soon as it opened.

The footman called after him. "Begging your pardon, Mr. Colson, but Mr. Dibley wants to see you in the main parlor."

Tremain gave a quick nod to Treves and headed down the hall. Entering the room, he slammed the door behind him. "I suppose Eliza informed you what happened in the village? Where is she? I must explain."

Jon shook his head. "Miss Winston didn't tell me much, but I guessed something dramatic transpired since she came back alone and in tears. And I assumed you would follow. She did say a woman called you Hawkestone."

Tremain sat in the nearby chair, and Jon sat opposite. "Lady Samantha Trimly."

Jon winced. "Well, how unfortunate. I never understood what you saw in that harpy. So, your secret is out."

Tremain leaned his cane against the chair, then ran his hands through his hair in frustration. "Samantha has vowed to spread malicious gossip through London society."

Jon crossed his arms. "From the longing gazes you and Miss Winston had exchanged, I'd assumed your relationship moved toward the intimate."

"Yes."

"Then why did you not tell her about yourself? I do hate to be the one to say I told you so—"

"Go ahead. I deserve it. In my selfish attempt to repair what's broken, I've exposed my family to scandal, and I may have lost the woman I love."

"Love? Well, that explains the depth of Miss Winston's despair. I would suggest you leave her be for the moment. Emotions are running high. Letting things simmer for the rest of the day would be wise. However, there is one other person you must tell. Andrew Payne."

Tremain slumped in his chair. What a muddle. "Have him brought to me, and Jon, I believe now would be the time to engage a young curate or priest to take my place. I will confess all to my parishioners at the conclusion of Sunday services this week. I've made a complete mess of this, haven't I?"

"Yes, but with the best intentions. Though I didn't initially agree with your stratagem, I understood your reasons and admired you all the more for them. I must admit it did help. You assisted others and healed in the process, or how else would you have allowed love to enter your heart?"

"I should have listened to you. After all, you warned me it could end badly. And it has. How arrogant of me."

Jon stood. "I'll fetch the lad."

Jon soon returned, motioning to Drew to take the seat opposite Tremain. Jon gave him a reassuring smile and left the room.

"Have you seen Miss Winston?" Tremain asked.

Drew nodded. "She said she wasn't feeling well and went to her room."

Tremain cringed. Jon was right, now would not be the time to confront her. "I have something to tell you, Drew. Before I became a priest, I was in the army, a captain in the Twenty-Fourth Regiment of Foot. I was injured during a scuffle with Zulu warriors and was in the thick of things at the Battle of Rorke's Drift in South Africa. Ever hear of it?" Drew's eyes were wide, and he shook his head. How to explain all this to a nine-year-old child?

"I hurt my leg and suffered grievous wounds to my heart and soul. When I recovered, I left the army and entered the church, which was to be my original career when I was younger. I wanted to help others and, in turn, help myself. But in doing so, I kept my real identity secret. I see now how self-centered it was of me."

Tremain waited to see if Drew absorbed any of this. "Then, who are you?" he asked.

"I am Viscount Hawkestone, second son of the Duke of Gransford."

Drew gulped. "You're The Hawk? Really?"

"Yes. I'm sorry. I should have told you before this."

Drew's expressive blue eyes lit up with excitement. "Does that mean you'll be living here?"

Tremain never considered that particular wrinkle. "Yes. I'll be leaving my post immediately."

Drew bounded from his chair and threw himself in Tremain's arms. "Then we can be the best of friends."

Tremain embraced the boy tightly. "The very best."

As Jon said, he'd let love into his heart—and this lad was a big part of it. When all was said and done, Drew may be the only person happy that he was Hawkestone.

A sobering thought.

ELIZA STAYED IN HER room the rest of the day, forgoing dinner, though Mrs. Hughes had sent up a small tray with bread, cheese, and fruit, which she picked at. She indulged in a good, cleansing cry—not something she engaged in much, but Eliza sorely needed the emotional outlay.

Forget how mortifying it had been to come face-to-face with one of Tremain's former mistresses. To find out he was not merely a clergyman but the son of a duke. Viscount Hawkestone, no less, her employer and benefactor.

Eliza had surmised that his upper-class accent resulted from his time in the army—and his education. Didn't one go to university to become a clergyman? She'd assumed he came from a middle-class environment. The son of a doctor or barrister, perhaps. Above her station, to be sure, but not out of the realm of possibility. The belief she could be a partner to an educated vicar was terrible enough, but to align herself with a viscount? The son of a duke?

It could *not* happen.

It wasn't done nor accepted by anyone from *any* class. What lay between them was over. How could Tremain not tell her? Clenching her fist, Eliza held it to her chest. Her heart broke. She'd fallen in love—and nothing could ever come of it.

Eliza sat upright. She was to go to him tonight. There was nothing else for it. She *must* resign from her position. What if he moved into the manor house? She would be there as his employee. How awkward would that be?

Best to cut it clean.

Dashing away a few wayward tears from her cheek, she reached for her cloak and slipped it on. One of the worst things to endure from this horrid mess? She would have to leave Drew, which would hurt almost as much as saying goodbye to Tremain. She adored the lad. After stepping out into the dim hallway, she hurried down the stairs.

Lifting her skirts, she ran to the vicarage. Best to do this now while she possessed the courage. Eliza pounded frantically on the door, and it opened. Tremain stood in the doorway dressed in black trousers and a white shirt. Blast the man for being so appealing.

"I didn't think you would come," he said, his voice low.

"I'm not staying. I have something to say."

Tremain stepped aside. "Then you had best come in and say it."

Taking a few steps into the room, she ventured no farther into the parlor. Eliza met his gaze. The cold mask was firmly in place. Then she could do the same. Say her piece and walk away.

"Tomorrow, I'll be writing to the Governesses Benevolent Institution to advertise for a replacement for me, though I will stay in the position until you find a suitable candidate. I require a good reference, your lordship."

He flinched at the word 'lordship.' "If you would let me explain—"

"There is nothing to explain. Logically, I can understand the reasons for your lie. However, when things between us grew serious and intimate, why did you not tell me everything before you took me to your bed? Do you think so little of me? Did I not deserve the truth of your true identity to make a reasonable decision?"

"Yes. You deserved the truth. I am sorry."

Contrite, Eliza would give him that. "Thank you for the apology. Whatever was between us is now at an end. Surely you see, it cannot continue. A penniless, orphan governess and the son of a duke, a viscount in his own right? It simply isn't done." She was amazed she managed to keep her voice steady.

"You must do what you think is best." His tone sounded frostier than hers.

"The vicar with the frozen heart has returned. Very well. Goodbye, your lordship." Eliza gave him a stiff, formal curtsy and turned to leave.

"You wish to end it like this? You will not allow me to explain?" Eliza could hear the vulnerability in his voice. It made her pause, but she remained resolute.

"Yes. I wish to end it *exactly* like this. I thank you for everything you did for me. Goodbye—Trey." She slipped out the door and ran toward the estate, tears trailing down her cheeks.

He did not come after her. He did not hold her there and force her to listen to his varied reasons for his deception.

Instead, Tremain let her go.

And that hurt worse than the subterfuge itself.

Chapter 22

AS TREMAIN STOOD BEFORE his congregation, his nerves tingled as if facing a tribe of Zulus. If any of the villagers had heard the exchange outside the pub a few days ago, he hadn't heard of it.

All sang the service's final hymn, "Praise my Soul, the Kingdom of Heaven." As the organist wheezed out the final chords, Tremain raised his hand to halt their departure.

"A moment of your time, please. I wish to announce I'll be stepping down immediately as the priest of this parish." A low rumble moved through the crowd. "Mr. Dibley has already found a suitable replacement, a young man of good and pious character eager to serve. He has my blessing. I hope next week you will welcome the Reverend Lucien Stephens warmly. As for myself, I stand humbly before you to ask forgiveness. I did not present myself honestly to you all."

Tremain hesitated. Every pair of eyes in the church riveted on him. "I came here a damaged and broken veteran of the Anglo-Zulu War. And you welcomed me regardless of my demeanor. When I reached my age of majority, I intended to enter the church but turned to the army instead. At the lowest ebb of my life, I turned back to my faith. Though I *am* a clergyman, I didn't give you my full name or the truth of my identity. I stand before you, Tremain Bennett Colson Hornsby, Viscount Hawkestone, second son of the Duke of Gransford."

Shocked gasps rose from the crowd, and the church grew eerily silent. Tremain cleared his throat. Sweat ran down the valley of his spine, but he continued, "I intend to take up my seat as viscount and landlord—if it is in your good graces to allow me to do so. I wish nothing more than to continue to serve this village. I pray for God's strength, kindness, and forgiveness and your continued health and happiness. Thank you."

As Tremain clasped his cane, he stepped from the pulpit. Each time his cane hit the floor, a thump reverberated through the small church as he descended the aisle. The impact of his deception hit him hard. He'd played with others' lives to soothe his own.

He passed the first pew. The men touched their forelocks and murmured, "My lord." The women said the same, only they curtsied. Most gave him warm smiles. Tremain's eyes grew moist. He caught a glimpse of a gray cloak. Was Eliza here? Surely, he imagined it.

While he stood at the open doors, the organist played another hymn, and the congregation exited the church.

Jacob Treacher held out his hand, and Tremain took it. "Thank you, your lordship, for everything you've done as vicar and viscount. This village will not forget your food and seed donations, prayers, and goodwill. I welcome you to Hawksgreen, Viscount Hawkestone."

Tremain shook his hand. It was hard to keep the emotion from his voice. "Thank you, Jacob. I plan to work closely with Mr. Stephens and Mr. Dibley to see to the continued care of everyone living in and around Hawksgreen."

Men standing in close proximity nodded their heads in agreement. As the last of his parishioners drifted away, Tremain stood humbled by their forgiveness and compassion. Would his family and those of his class be as merciful?

His family, yes.

The rest of society? Unlikely.

Eliza?

No, and he could not fault her. She would be leaving, and her upcoming departure left a gaping hole in his heart that would never mend.

ELIZA HURRIED TOWARD the manor. When she'd heard from Mr. Dibley that Tremain would inform the congregation of his true identity, she could not stay away. She'd slipped in during the final moments of the service and witnessed his deeply felt plea for forgiveness. It touched her heart. And part of her forgave him as well.

He looked magnificent in the white and black robes. Watching him limp down the aisle as the villagers gave him the veneration he deserved nearly caused her heart to burst with pride. Eliza escaped before he saw her standing at the back of the church.

Regardless of her forgiveness in whatever amount, none of this changed her mind. It merely solidified her reasons for departing. Watching everyone say 'my lord' proved it. Breathlessly, she stepped across the threshold of the front entrance. Eliza realized she should've used the rear door. Though she was hardly thinking straight, her mind whirled with conflicting emotions.

Eliza sprinted past Treves only to have Mr. Dibley step in her path. "May I speak with you a moment, Miss Winston? In the study?"

Reluctantly, she followed him into the room. Mr. Dibley closed the door, then motioned her to sit before the desk.

"Miss Winston—Eliza—if ever there was a flawed, stubborn man, it is Tremain. I should know. We grew up together." He sat in his chair and leaned forward, his elbows resting on the desk. "I told him from the beginning his plan could, in fact, hurt others as well as himself. But he would not hear it. His sincere desire to atone for whatever happened in South Africa overrode all logical thought. I could not deny him his request, and nor could his family. He pleaded with us, stating his very soul was in jeopardy. How could we refuse?"

"H-h-he told me what happened in South Africa."

Mr. Dibley sat back, his look incredulous. "Did he, indeed? None of us could persuade him to confide. I'm glad he told someone and doubly glad it was you."

She pulled off her gloves. "Mr. Dibley—"

"Please, call me Jon."

Eliza gave him a shaky smile. "Jon, the fact remains he didn't tell me of his true self. But beyond that, you must know there can be nothing between us."

Jon shrugged. "I know of no such thing. Why? Because you're supposedly beneath him, according to society? Those who care about you and Tremain will make no such distinctions."

"But his family, the duke—"

"Are delightful people. I lost my mother at a young age; there was only my father and I. He's steward to the duke, and I was given free run of the house and grew up with Tremain and his two brothers, Spencer and Harrison. I attended university with Tremain, all paid by the duke. Never was I made to feel like a servant but rather part of the family. Believe me, when I tell you, they will welcome you with open arms."

Oh, how she wanted to believe such a fairy tale. A lump of emotion lodged in her throat. All of this was so perplexing; her mind churned with conflicting thoughts.

What to do?

"Shall I tell you how accepting the duke and his family are?" Jon continued. "Spencer, the youngest brother, has just announced he's to be married. The lady in question ran a brothel."

Eliza's eyes widened in surprise. "A brothel? Truly?"

Jon nodded. "As far as society dictates, she is not an ideal wife for the son of a duke, but I assure you that the family would accept any woman Spencer chose, regardless of background. They haven't met her yet, but if Spencer loves her, that is enough for them. The Hornsbys are a rare sort to be found in the aristocracy. They are rich and powerful but believe in service and assisting those less fortunate. Nor are they judgmental."

He gave her a warm smile. "They would accept you. Talk with Tremain. If you truly wish to have a future with him, I'm afraid you will have to make the first overture knowing his stubborn nature as I do. None of us want you to leave. Tremain most of all, though he may not show it." Jon laughed gently. "Since we were lads, he's always done that. If anything overwhelmed him, he retreated behind his mask. Surely, you know that Tremain is *not* a cold man at the core."

Eliza dashed away the tear that had trickled down her cheek. "No, he's not cold. I will think about what you said." She stood. "I must see to the arrangements for Drew's birthday celebration." At the door, she turned and gave Jon a warm smile. "Thank you. You're a true friend. To both of us."

IT WAS SUNDAY AND DREW'S birthday celebration. Eliza's breath caught when Tremain walked into the room. He no longer wore his collar and black coat. Instead, he wore a fashionable brown suit that bespoke his aristocratic status. Their eyes met only a few times, and she stayed well away from him before and during the dinner as she still had much to think about. Yes, she was weakening slightly, but common sense still dictated there could be nothing between, regardless of Jon Dibley's assurances otherwise.

The food was delicious, and it warmed Eliza's heart to see people from different classes talking freely and enjoying a meal together. Perhaps a ray of hope for her and Tremain, or was it merely wishful thinking?

Mrs. Hughes brought the chocolate cake and sat it before a smiling Drew. Everyone sang "For He's a Jolly Good Fellow" and clapped as Drew blew out the ten candles on the cake.

Eliza smiled warmly. "Now, Drew. You have a choice before you. Would you like to open your gifts first or have the cake?"

"Gifts first, please!"

Everyone laughed and moved toward the parlor. Eliza sat next to Drew and handed him the parcels. Tremain, leaning on his cane, stood well back from the others, his heated gaze firm on her. Fissions of awareness swept across her skin.

The Tompkinses and the servants banded together to give Drew a beautiful set of toy soldiers. Jon Dibley gave him a collection of fine marbles. Eliza gave him two books, *The Life and Adventures of Robinson Crusoe* and *The Rose and the Ring*, adventure stories that would appeal to a boy of ten years.

Tremain stepped forward. Drew looked up at him.

"I have a gift for you, Drew. At least I hope you will see it as a gift. The main reason I became a priest was to help others. But perhaps I only made things worse. It was not my intent."

Drew shook his head emphatically. "No. You didn't make things worse. You helped my mum. She told me she would've been lost if it wasn't for you—and the viscount. You helped *me*. I've got a home now. Friends. You helped Miss Winston. She told me you saved her from robbers. I'm glad you're The Hawk—*and* the vicar." Drew beamed up at him, and Eliza's heart clenched in her chest.

Tremain laid a hand on Drew's shoulder. "Thank you. You're a good lad. My gift to you? To become my son. You can even have my name, but only if you wish."

Drew's brows furrowed. "What is your name?"

"Tremain Bennett Colson Hornsby. You can be Drew Payne or whatever name you wish."

"Andrew Hornsby." Drew mulled it over. "I like it. The name Payne is not really mine. My mum told me once she'd picked it because she suffered nothing but pain all her life. 'Except you, my dear one,' she'd

said. I'd just as soon take yours, Vicar. I mean—your lordship—what
do I call you?"

Eliza was captivated by the conversation between Drew and
Tremain, and, glancing about the room, she could see everyone else was
as well.

"You may call me Tremain. Or my friends call me Trey. Or uncle—"

"Uncle Trey. I like that. Someday, can I call you—Father?"

Tremain's eyes glittered with emotion. "Whenever you're ready."

"I've never had a father," Drew whispered.

Tremain smiled. "Well, you have one now."

Drew threw his arms around Tremain's waist, and there wasn't a dry
eye in the room. A cynical person may scoff at such a heartwarming
scene, but Eliza understood how it benefited both man and boy. As
everyone headed to the dining room for cake, Tremain gently gripped
Eliza's wrist, halting her.

"Can you give me a few moments?" he murmured.

"Yes." Her heart stuttered in her chest at his touch. Apprehension
rolled through her as she was not in any frame of mind for a serious
conversation.

He let his hand drop. "I ask you not to resign. Not yet. Tonight, I'm
heading south to my family's estate in Hastings. Except for my brother
Spence, we're reuniting. He'll join us later. I've not seen my family in
two years. I pushed them away as I did everyone else. I have amends to
make." His voice was officious and detached. Very well, she could do
the same. Unfortunately, she was as stubborn as he was.

"I'm not sure what that has to do with me," she replied.

"It's in Drew's best interest to have you remain as his governess. If
that means I stay away from Hawksgreen and the estate, I can arrange
it."

Eliza blinked at him in shock. "But you told the villagers you would
take up your duties here."

"Ah," he said softly. "So it *was* you I saw leaving the church." Eliza flushed but didn't reply. "Regardless, I can easily see to my duties from Hastings. It's not far, and communication is possible through letters and telegraphs. Besides, I must allow people to become used to the new priest. Or perhaps I need to become used to the idea that the vicar and viscount are the same person. I must come to terms with what I've done before, during, and most decidedly after the war."

Tremain took her hand, his thumb rubbing across the top, causing heat to spread throughout her. "I'm sorry you were subjected to Lady Trimly. She's a part of my sordid past, one I would rather forget. I ask one thing from you. If you decide to stay for Drew, please do not dismiss what's between us. There could be much more." The coldness from his voice had disappeared.

Eliza shook her head. "More between us? No, I don't see how. I suppose I should be angrier that you didn't trust me with the truth, but this isn't about me. It's you—how you must have suffered. The war damaged you, without a doubt. You need to mend in your own way, I understand. But a viscount? There are too many obstacles to us being together. But I will stay for now. For Drew."

Tremain kissed her hand and, without a word, left the room. How she wanted him to say that he loved her. But he didn't. Yes, this parting was best.

Then why did her heart ache so much?

Chapter 23

TREMAIN HAD BEEN AT Gransford Manor for nearly three weeks and, in that time, moved no closer to a solution or decision regarding Eliza and the rest of his life. A cold cup of tea and a plate of half-eaten beefsteak sandwiches sat beside him.

One conclusion he reached: he had made a grave error keeping his family at arm's length. How he'd missed them. During childhood, he, his brothers, and Jon had free run of the estate. They were not wholly ill-behaved, but his parents had allowed them to be children. Tremain soon discovered that was a rarity when he'd visited the staid homes of some of the lads from school.

Once he reached the age of majority, his mother and father patiently listened to his reasons for not entering the church and bought him a commission in the army as requested. They allowed him to live his life, make mistakes, and find his own path. For that, he was eternally grateful. Now they had welcomed him home with open arms and hearts when they should call him to task for withdrawing entirely from the family. They supported and loved him unconditionally. He did not deserve his family any more than he deserved Eliza.

Ah. Eliza.

Sighing, Tremain reached for a sandwich wedge and nibbled at it absently. One of the main reasons for his departure from Hawksgreen was to give Eliza time to adjust to the revelation of his identity.

Would she forgive him? As of his latest communication with Jon, she was still there. But how long would she remain?

In the telegram, Jon had urged him to return to take up his duties as viscount and to resolve other outstanding issues. His friend was right. As always. How strange that as a vicar, Tremain could dispense advice and common sense but had none for himself.

Harrison strode into the room. They looked much alike with their dark looks and silver-gray eyes, but his older brother was a few inches shorter, hovering under six feet in height.

"Don't get up, Brother." Harrison winked.

"I wasn't planning to."

Harrison gave a bark of laughter as he sunk into the chair opposite. "Ah, beefsteak. Excellent." He grabbed a piece and ate it heartily.

"Harry, I wanted to ask, what have you been up to the past several months? There have been no letters. You used to be a proficient letter writer."

"You haven't exactly written any either, Brother."

"No, I apologize again. That will change. Along with other aspects of my life."

The corner of his brother's mouth quirked sardonically. "Stepping out of the shadows? Leaving the darkness behind? Ready to join the land of the living?"

"Something like that. No need to mock. I know I've mucked this up," Tremain snapped.

"Easy. Call it a gentle admonishment. You're here now. I'm glad to have my brother back."

"You didn't answer my question."

Harrison snatched up a small sugar biscuit and popped it in his mouth. "What I've been up to? Keeping busy. The ladies, you know. My mistress in particular. She keeps me in a perpetual state of exhaustion."

Tremain snorted. Something was off about his brother's statement. It didn't ring true, as if Harrison had secrets. Tremain knew all about secrets —and telling falsehoods.

"But beyond all that," his brother continued. "Parliament calls, and duty beckons. I'll be heading to London the day after tomorrow."

When Tremain became a viscount, the Queen ennobled Harrison, which meant that even though the Marquess of Tennington was a courtesy title, he could serve in the House of Lords alongside their father.

"Is Father going with you?" Tremain asked.

"No. Not this time." Harry popped the last piece of sandwich in his mouth, then reached for a napkin, wiping his fingers.

Strange. Their father never missed a session.

"There have been a few developments while you were off being a dedicated priest," Harrison said. "We didn't want to say anything, as it only came to light two months ago. Father has a slight heart problem."

"How slight? And why wasn't I told as soon as I arrived?" his voice rose in annoyance.

"Curb that short temper of yours, please. It's not *that* serious. Father sometimes experiences a racing heart, and because of it, he will have to curb certain activities. He will be going to London less, that's all. I can step in and see to our interests. Besides, it's not a death sentence, and he certainly isn't an invalid." Harrison popped another piece of a sandwich in his mouth and swallowed. "I discovered it during an examination. Father was complaining of shortness of breath. I called in his physician, and he concurred with my diagnosis."

Harrison had studied medicine at university but never pursued it, though considering his status in society, Tremain supposed he couldn't. As the heir to a duke, the noble profession would be regarded as beneath him. It was a shame, as he remembered how animated and alive his brother had been when discussing what he'd learned.

"Harry, I have the distinct feeling mankind has suffered because you didn't become a physician," Tremain said, his voice soft.

Harrison flushed but didn't acknowledge the statement. "We did not want to burden you with Father's medical news the moment you walked through the door. All it means is that I'll have to take up the slackened reins, as it were."

Tremain frowned. "You *are* sure it's not serious? That you're not placating me in light of my fragile emotional state?"

Harrison snorted. "You? Fragile? Not even at your lowest ebb. And no, I'm not pacifying you at all. You know me better than that."

"We are all getting old; it seems," Tremain murmured.

"Yes. Father is fifty-eight but is otherwise fit and healthy. He will have to be prudent." Harrison crossed his legs. "And at thirty-three, soon to be thirty-four, I suppose I should start looking for a suitable wife to continue the line. Which brings us to *you*."

"Enough, Harrison. Leave your brother alone."

Both men turned to see their mother standing by the fireplace. Though threads of gray were visible in her chestnut brown hair, and she'd gained a few more wrinkles since Tremain had seen her last, she was still elegant, beautiful, and every inch the duchess. Both men stood, though it took Tremain a little longer to reach his feet.

"Harrison, be a darling, run along and see to your packing. Your valet is all in a dither and needs your guidance. Also, see that a fresh pot of tea and sandwiches are brought to me."

Harrison kissed his mother's cheek. "Go easy on him, Mother dear." With a salute, his brother departed.

The duchess sat in the chair Harrison just vacated. "Has Harrison told you?"

"About Father? Yes. Though I suppose I've no right to be annoyed considering my actions."

"No need to bring it up, my dear. We understood though we missed you terribly. There have been too many separations. Your various campaigns as a soldier, your time in the church. But you are here now."

That was just what Harrison had said. "I've missed you all as well. Time to move forward," Tremain replied.

Two footmen entered the room, swiftly removed the old tray, then replaced it with another holding a pot of tea, two cups, and plates of sandwiches and cakes.

"You may go and close the door behind you," his mother said to the servants.

The footmen bowed, and one replied, "Your Grace."

Once alone, his mother poured them tea, then passed Tremain a plate full of sandwiches and cakes. "There, tuck in. You always had a hearty appetite. Do you still?"

"No, not as much as before, but for you...I shall make an effort."

The duchess sipped her tea. "I must say, since giving birth to the three of you, my life has been anything but dull. You are all astounding men in your own right, and I couldn't be prouder of any of you. Especially you, Tremain."

She chuckled softly. "You could be the most sensitive of the three, though Spencer certainly had his moments. When emotions became overpowering, you would withdraw. You still do, and I innately understood why you had to extract yourself from society and family. We *all* understood."

"I'm eternally grateful for your support and love," Tremain murmured.

"Did it help, my dear? Being a priest?"

Tremain bit into his sandwich, waiting a few moments before he answered. "Yes. I'm on the right path for recovery, both physically and emotionally, and, in all honesty, spiritually. It's a beginning. I've always considered myself more spiritual than religious."

"Concerning the young boy, Andrew Payne. You mentioned that you were going to make him your ward."

Tremain nodded. "I'll be going one step further. I intend to adopt him. He's agreed and will be taking the family name. There are no actual lawful steps to take since adoption is not legal. But I will have the solicitor put something down on paper anyway. "

His mother placed her cup and saucer on the tray, then met his gaze. "Oh my. I am to have a grandson?"

"You will love him, Mother. A bright, honest, and delightful boy."

"My. Your life *is* taking new and exciting directions. And what of love, Tremain? You have not spoken of Miss Eliza Winston since you arrived, though you mentioned her with some affection in your last letter?"

He would give his mother this; she waited until now to bring up Eliza. Why prevaricate? "I love her. Absolutely adore her. Eliza is intelligent, beautiful, and speaks her mind. I never thought to find a woman I would care to share my life with, but I have. However, I've made a complete hash of things. She found out about my identity in a rather crass way." He told the story of meeting Lady Trimly in the village, though he censored the more salacious details.

The duchess frowned as she picked up her cup and sipped her tea. "I never cared for that woman. We no sooner received your telegraph warning us your identity was compromised when the gossip reached us. She wasted no time in spreading her tale. Abominable woman. But I do not comment on my sons' mistresses, former or otherwise."

"Very prudent, Mother," Tremain's mouth quirked.

"I *cannot* understand why you still sit here, Tremain." His mother never called any of her sons by nicknames, and he found it endearing. "It is quite apparent your life awaits in Hawksgreen. Why delay? Go to your governess, my dear, and profess your undying love. Claim her and the young lad. Be a loving family. It is what you deserve."

She gave him an affectionate smile. "When the doctors released you from the hospital, you had us all quite worried. You could have taken to your rooms and drank and brooded as many do in the same circumstance. And who could blame them? Instead, you assessed how to begin the healing and followed through on it. *You* are my hero."

A lump of emotion lodged itself in Tremain's throat. Despite his pushing everyone away, they forgave him. Even admired him. "Mother—"

"Go to Eliza and Drew. Tell them how you feel. Tell them everything. Be happy."

He stood before his mother, took her hand, and kissed it. "Thank you. For understanding. For loving me. You and Father both. I will go. Immediately."

ELIZA'S INSIDES WERE in knots. Staring out the carriage window at the serene countryside didn't settle her nerves. According to the driver, Gransford Manor was no more than a three-hour trip. The journey was undertaken for Drew's sake, as the lad suffered from Tremain's absence. Drew seemed to wither without Tremain. Truth? She suffered as well.

In the three weeks since his departure, Eliza had plenty to think about. Her mind constantly returned to one particular revelation: Tremain's younger brother was about to marry a woman of supposed ill repute. Jon had said that Spencer Hornsby was somewhat eccentric and would go off for months at a time and lose himself in research. His peers often ridiculed him for his solitary personality, and his brothers, especially Tremain, often protected him.

If Tremain's family would readily accept Philomena McGrattan, sight unseen, why not a governess? She had to hand it to Spencer Hornsby for reaching out for love regardless of societal norms and the consequences of breaching them. Eliza admired Philomena for doing the same.

Regardless of all the drama surrounding Tremain's former mistress and his real identity, what she cared about was Tremain.

How she loved him.

Under the solitary exterior lay a passionate, compassionate man who had captured her heart.

And she could not stay away from him another minute.

"Are we there yet?" Drew asked, practically bouncing in his seat.

She was not the only one excited at the prospect of seeing Tremain. Perhaps she should have sent word she was coming, but Jon had encouraged her to surprise him.

Eliza patted Drew's arm affectionately. "Another hour at least."

Drew sighed. "My mates said the vicar is mean, cold as a fish. It's one of the reasons we fought that day."

"We both know that's not true, don't we?" Eliza said, her voice gentle. "He has a heart; only it's been hiding behind a protective wall."

"Like a moat? Like on one of those old castles we've been studying?"

Eliza smiled. "Yes, like a moat."

"We'll help him, won't we, miss?"

"I think we have already. Why don't you try to nap? You had no sleep last night, and if you nap, we'll be there the next time you awake. Lay down on the seat opposite."

Drew did, and she covered him with the throw. He soon drifted off into a deep sleep.

The last time Eliza was in this carriage with Tremain, she had straddled him, rubbing against him as they clutched each other tight—kissing wildly. Her heart sped up at the sensual memory as she laid a hand on her chest as if to try and stem its erratic beat.

Heavens.

If she was reluctant to become a vicar's wife, the apprehension increased at the thought of becoming a viscount's lady. Would he even propose? But regardless of the possible obstacles, Eliza loved him enough to toss aside all fears. It just took a while to come to that conclusion.

She had tried to pass the time reading as they traveled but read the same page more than once. Drew continued to sleep. Abruptly, the carriage came to a halt. The driver, Terrance, slid the window open and peered in. Eliza immediately put her finger to her mouth and pointed at Drew.

"Where are we? What's happened?" Eliza spoke in a hushed tone.

"We be in Staplecross, and there be a delay. You might want to stretch your legs, Miss Winston, begging your pardon," Terrance answered in as low a voice as hers. "I'll try and find out what's going on."

He slid the window shut, then opened the door to assist her from the coach. There was a long line of halted carriages going in both directions. As she was about to step down, her breath caught. A man in a carriage farther down heading the opposite way stood on the wrought iron stair, gauging the situation.

Tremain.

He looked handsome in a gray traveling coat, his head bare, the breeze tousling his raven-black locks. Her heart nearly ceased to beat when his gaze met hers.

Every wayward and questioning emotion came into crystalline clearness.

Eliza truly loved him more than life itself.

A slow smile crept across Tremain's sensual lips, and his eyes softened. Eliza could not contain Her complete joy at seeing him. Eliza waved, smiling, ignoring Terrance's offer to help her down. Instead, she jumped to the ground in a most unladylike manner.

Eliza searched frantically for Tremain, pushing through the people standing about the parked carriages. It shouldn't be hard to locate him as Tremain stood head and shoulders above every other man. At last, she found him in the middle of the thoroughfare, leaning on his cane and smiling broadly. Blast decorum and proper manners, she ran to him, stopping before him breathlessly.

"Eliza. Where were you heading?" His voice was low and husky and full of emotion.

"I...we...Drew is napping in the carriage. He was having trouble sleeping and eating, you see. He missed you dreadfully." Eliza laid her hand on her chest, trying to catch her breath.

Tremain's eyebrow arched questioningly. "Did he, indeed? And you, Miss Winston?"

"I've missed you, too. Where were *you* going?"

Tremain gently lifted her hand to his mouth. Neither wore gloves. "Home to Hawksgreen. To you and my son." His warm lips roved across her knuckles, causing her knees to buckle. "I've missed you, too—both of you. Come home? With me?" He turned her hand over and passionately kissed her palm, causing her to shudder with desire. "I love you, Eliza. I cannot live without you. Please do not ask me to try; it will be my finish. Put an end to my misery and be my wife. My lady. My lover and friend in all things."

Tears fell freely down her cheeks. "Yes, I will marry you. I cannot live without you, Trey, you glorious, stubborn, and wonderful man. I love you so much."

His cane fell to the ground as he pulled her close and gave her a devastating kiss. A few people tsked and gasped in shock, but one man shouted, "Well done."

"Uncle Trey!"

Eliza and Tremain broke apart at the sound of Drew's voice. He ran toward them and threw himself into Tremain's arms. Tremain lifted him and hugged him back.

"You came to get us. We were coming to *you*," Drew exclaimed happily.

"I've missed you, lad: you and Miss Winston both. In fact, if it's all right with you, she has agreed to marry me, if you can imagine it. What do you say, Drew? Could you stand to be gaining a mother and a father?"

Drew looked back and forth between them, a large smile on his face. "Yes! What happens now?"

Tremain laughed. "Well, we can climb into my carriage and head to Gransford Manor for the night. Or we can stay two or three nights. It's not far, and my parents are eager to meet you both. We'll have Terrance follow us. What do you say, my dears? After all, this should be a family vote."

Eliza's heart was bursting with love. "Yes!" both she and Drew cried.

Tremain kissed Drew on the forehead and then lowered him to the ground. Drew picked up his cane.

About to move forward, Eliza halted Tremain, clasped his hand, and kissed it. "I love you, Trey. With everything I am. With everything I ever hope to be."

He whispered in her ear, "And you melt my heart and soothe my soul. Come, let us love and live."

With those words, Eliza knew he would never again be the vicar with the frozen heart.

EPILOGUE

THREE WEEKS LATER

TREMAIN, ELIZA, AND Drew stayed at Gransford Manor for an extended visit. His parents had insisted. But it was time to make plans, and once afternoon tea concluded, Tremain managed to get Eliza alone in the library. He kissed her passionately but reluctantly ended it as he had much to discuss with her. They sat together on the sofa.

"Father spoke to me this morning before breakfast. He suggested that I make an appearance at Parliament. I agreed. If I am to take on the mantle of Viscount Hawkestone, best to start by fulfilling my obligation in the House of Lords."

Eliza frowned. "You'll be leaving us?"

"Not for long. For two weeks at most. Loving you has helped me heal, but I need to do more. I want to do all I can for war veterans. Too many are forgotten, tossed aside, allowed to live a life of poverty not worthy of their sacrifice."

"Oh, it's a wonderful cause. Yes, I completely agree."

Tremain pulled a letter from his coat pocket and held it up. "To change the subject. Spencer has written, and he has an idea that I wish to convey to you. I'll leave the decision up to you."

She smiled. "Now, you have piqued my curiosity."

"He suggests a double wedding. That we exchange vows here at the manor at the same time as he and Philomena, it will be a small and private affair in the third week of May unless you would rather have a larger gathering in a church. Anything you want, my love."

"A small family affair sounds wonderful. Let's do it," Eliza said, her voice soft.

"I'll tell Mother. She will be pleased. And I'll write Spencer that his plan is a good one." Tremain slipped the letter into his pocket.

"And where will Drew and I go? Back to Hawksgreen?"

"You could, or you can stay here until the wedding. Perhaps you would like a break from my family."

Eliza chucked. "I adore your parents. And Drew is having the time of his life. We'll stay here. Drew can continue his lessons, and I can continue my own lessons. Your mother is instructing me on the ways of society and being a lady."

"God, how tedious," Tremain groaned.

"Perhaps, but I find it useful. We are making it fun. Lots of tea and cakes and browsing catalogs. Your mother said that she always had wanted a daughter." Eliza's lower lip trembled. "I always wanted a mother—and a family."

Tremain embraced her. "You have one now, my love."

"Where will you stay in London?" Eliza asked.

"The family has a town house in Mayfair. I'll stay there. Also, I will have Harry there to show me about Parliament."

Harrison had been in London for the past two weeks. Perhaps Tremain would discover just what secrets his older brother was keeping. Something was up, and Tremain was determined to discover it.

How to convince his brother to hold out for true love instead of being led by duty and obligation? An arranged marriage was not for Harrison. Tremain felt it to his bones.

Now he had to persuade Harrison to see it in the same light.

Yes, Harrison deserved to be loved.

~~~SEE A SNEAK PREVIEW of Harrison's story, *The Marquess of Secrets*, further along. A more detailed epilogue catching up with the brothers ten years later can be found at the conclusion of *The Marquess of Secrets*.

More Books by Karyn Gerrard

~HISTORICAL~

The Spinster and Mr. Glover The Revised Edition (Book #1 Blind Cupid Series)

The Governess and the Beast (Book #2 Blind Cupid Series)

The Copper and the Madam (Book #3 Blind Cupid Series)

Protecting the Duke (The Rakes of St. Regent's Park #1)

The Baron and the Mistress-Revised Edition (The Rakes of St. Regent's Park #2)

Knight of Christmas (The Rakes of St. Regent's Park #3)

Duke of Pain (The Rakes of St. Regent's Park #4)

Bold Seduction (of Professor Hornsby) (Book #1 Hornsby Brothers Series)

The Vicar's Frozen Heart (Book #2 Hornsby Brothers Series)

Marquess of Secrets (Book #3 Hornsby Brothers Series)

Beloved Monster (Book #1 The Ravenswood Chronicles)

Beloved Beast (Book #2 The Ravenswood Chronicles)

Marriage with a Proper Stranger (Book #1 Men of Wollstonecraft Hall Series)

Scandal with a Sinful Scot (Book #2 Men of Wollstonecraft Hall Series)

Love with a Notorious Rake (Book #3 Men of Wollstonecraft Hall Series)

The Not So Perfect Duke (The Rakes of St. Regent's Park #5)

COMING SOON! The Viscount of Shadows (The Rakes of St. Regent's Park #6)

~**Contemporary**~

My Highlander Cover Model (Heroes of Time Travel Anthology Series #1)

Timeless Heart (Heroes of Time Travel Anthology Series #2)

My Wicked Soul (It's Never Too Late for Love Anthology Series #1)

That Christmas Feeling (It's Never Too Late for Love Anthology Series #2)

Wild Pitch

He's the Wicked Bad (Wicked Men of Rockland City #1)

His Wicked Celtic Kiss (Wicked Men of Rockland City #2)

His Wicked Cold Heart (Wicked Men of Rockland City #3) is coming soon!

Author Biography

A MULTI-PUBLISHED AUTHOR from the East Coast of Canada, Karyn Gerrard loves to write sensual historical and contemporary romances. Tortured heroes are an absolute must.

Karyn's been happily married for a long time to her own hero. His encouragement and loving support keep her moving forward.

To learn more about Karyn and her books, visit www.karyngerrard.com[1]

Also, visit her on Facebook, Twitter, Pinterest, Instagram, and Bookbub.

"LOOKING FOR A SWOON-worthy read? You can't go wrong with the lovely and emotional romances from Karyn Gerrard." ~**Vanessa Kelly, USA Today Bestselling author**

"Karyn Gerrard writes very enjoyable, richly textured historical romances." ~**Kate Pearce, New York Times and USA Today Bestselling author**

---

1.   http://www.karyngerrard.com/

Sneak Peek of The Marquess of Secrets

(Book #3 in The Hornsby Brothers)

Chapter 1

APRIL 1882
London, England

HARRISON HORNSBY, THE Marquess of Tennington and heir to the Duke of Gransford, lay on his mistress's bed—wholly spent. A thin sheen of sweat covered his body. The session was vigorous and bittersweet, for this would be the last time he'd visit Francesca Whitten, his paramour of three years.

Harrison believed he was growing too old for such doings, considering he turned thirty-four two weeks past. It was better to end this association before initiating his search in society's marriage mart.

His unspoken obligation was to find an appropriate bride amongst the aristocracy, a woman with the carriage and grace to one day become his duchess—and to be the mother to his children. Such a task was a centuries-old tradition and expected within the peerage. It was all well and good that his two younger brothers, Spencer and Tremain, married for love. He would not and could not allow himself such a luxury.

A firm believer in duty and all it entails, Harrison alone stood as the future of his family name and title, and his choice of bride was paramount. Harrison held out for as long as he could, hoping to fall in love like his brothers. Yearning for a love match his parents enjoyed was always a gamble and infrequent amongst the aristocracy.

Francesca interrupted his thoughts by arching her foot and trailing it along the back of his leg and across his buttocks.

"I've always admired your muscular and very firm arse, Tennington," she purred. "You're in fine fettle for a man who spends his time sitting in Parliament. It is where you spend your time, is it not? You come here so rarely; I've begun to fashion all sorts of scenarios."

Her foot caressed him, stirring his arousal. Surprisingly, he was ready to go again, but there will be no acting on it.

"Pray tell, what scenarios?" Harrison murmured, struggling to stay awake regardless of his physical reaction. He should be taking his leave, but this was the first time in weeks that he had time to relax in any way.

"At first, I thought it might be another woman. But you're not the sort of man to engage in sensual deceptions, even if I am your mistress. Then I thought you had a family secreted away in an isolated hamlet on the other side of the country. Again, it's not in your personality. Regardless of the scandal, you would acknowledge any bastards."

"Yes, I would."

"Not that you would be so careless in your dealings to even have illegitimate children. You plan things meticulously. I concluded that you are as eccentric as the rest of your family." Her foot halted in its exploration. "Oh, I am sorry."

That killed his arousal. Tossing the silk sheet across his naked body, he turned and sat upright.

Eccentric. Well.

He was wide awake now. "What have you heard?"

Gossip and societal machinations annoyed Harrison to no end. Yet, they were all around him as society thrived on chatter, whether the tittle-tattle had merit or not.

No one dared to speak about scandalous intrigues before the Hornsby family. Not while Harrison's father, the Duke of Gransford, remained one of the queen's favorites. And a powerful force at court and in the House of Lords.

Francesca had the grace to blush. The crimson color of her cheeks matched the reddish shade of her hair. "I don't wish to end this glorious afternoon with an argument," she stated, her lower lip thrust out.

"I give you my word that I will keep a tight rein on my annoyance. Please, do tell." He crossed his arms, watching her closely.

With a sigh, she met his gaze. "It is said that your youngest brother, Lord Spencer Hornsby, is—mad, suffers fits and inappropriate emotional outbursts. Because of it, he has hidden away in a remote Wales location not to embarrass his family."

The fury growing inside Harrison was potent, but he struggled to conceal it. However, there was no denying Spence was—different.

From earliest childhood, Harrison observed how Spence struggled with managing his emotions and other personality quirks.

Doctors were called in. All agreed that the boy must be carted off to an asylum. To the duke's credit, he would not brook any such suggestion. His father could be a force to reckon with when pushed too far. Protecting the family took priority, and Harrison respected his father for taking such a stance.

Observing Spence's travails firsthand sparked Harrison's interest in the study of medicine. He was a registered physician with the Royal College of Physicians, with degrees from Cambridge, but, alas, being a peer would not allow him to open a public practice. According to society, it was not an accepted role for the heir to a duke. One must adhere to the blasted rules. But he kept up with the latest developments in medicine.

Harrison encouraged Spence to place a rigid routine in his life to keep the demons at bay. Doing chores or tasks a certain way at the same time of day placated Spence and lessened the outbursts. Also, focusing on one study—like his research into the ancient Byzantine Empire—calmed him.

His brows furrowed. All Harrison ever wanted was to protect his youngest brother, but no matter what he'd done to try and divert the gossip, Spence was laughed at and talked about regardless.

"My youngest brother is not mad, contrary to malicious chatter. As a matter of fact, he's to be married in May."

Francesca bit her lower lip.

"What?" he asked, dreading the response.

"I've heard his fiancée is a prostitute. Not that I'm judging, God forbid."

How in blasted hell had that information seeped out? To say Spence's and Tremain's choices of brides were outside the norm of so-called proper society was an understatement. Not that Harrison cared about their backgrounds, but all the best to his brothers and their soon-to-be brides.

All the more reason that Harrison must ensure his choice was beyond reproach. It was best to deflect any further scrutiny into his family's personal business.

His parents were tolerant and progressive in their thinking and accepted both women warmly, but Harrison was well aware that the constant gossip hurt them, particularly his mother.

"I can trust you to keep this to yourself?" he ventured.

Francesca crossed her heart and nodded. "Absolutely. I'm known for my discretion. Though others do not hesitate to tell me things, I reveal nothing." She snuggled under the bedspread, and her eyes brightened with anticipation.

It was true; her tactfulness was one of the reasons he'd chosen her for his mistress.

"The week between Christmas and New Year, two of Spencer's friends hired a prostitute as a birthday gift. The madam herself took the assignment. Long story short, the week alone at a snowbound lodge in Wales resulted in a proposal. They are to be married next month."

Francesca smiled. "Falling in love in one week! How utterly romantic! Have you met her?"

He had, not two weeks past. The family gathered at Gransford Manor so he could meet not only Philomena McGrattan, the ex-madam, but Tremain's fiancée, Eliza Winston, the ex-governess. Philomena's gentle guidance and empathetic nature calmed Spence, and he focused all his restless energy on her, and she reveled in it.

A good match in all ways.

Harrison had believed that Spence, for all his foibles, would never find someone to love and love him in return. How gratifying that he had.

"Yes. For all of Philomena's tragic back story, she is a lady of courage and compassion. I am well pleased for my brother."

She smiled warmly. "Then I'm glad. I don't like repeating this prattle, but I suppose you should be aware, as no one would dare say it to your face."

True enough.

"But you will?"

"Well, yes. I genuinely *like* you, Tennington. I cannot say as such with all the men that have been in my life." She cuddled close to him and ran her fingertip along his lower lip. "Though you come here far too infrequently, I enjoy it when you do."

"I did tell you to take on another if you wished," Harrison said.

"No, I don't juggle multiple men. Besides, the older I've become, the more I enjoy the solitude between your visits. And you're most generous. I have no complaints about renting this town house, the servants, the horse, the carriage, and extra money." She drew her hand away and gave him another brilliant smile. "Besides the energetic bed sport, I like that you stay and talk. Take a meal. Oh, do you wish for me to ring for food? I ordered a platter of sliced meats be available, along with assorted cheeses, fruit, and fresh bread."

Tempting, but Harrison was not staying long enough to partake of food. "Perhaps later. Pray continue with the Hornsby gossip. I am all attention."

"Are you certain?"

Hell, it must be bad.

"Yes. I have steeled myself for what comes."

"It is said that your middle brother, Tremain, perpetuated a scam for his own selfish needs. He pretended to be a country vicar for a nefarious purpose. Since his war injuries have rendered him impotent, he took in a street urchin as his son."

That, as they say, takes the cake. Unbelievable. Again, Harrison's blood boiled. He took a deep breath and exhaled, hoping to contain his exasperation.

"Tremain is a hero of the Anglo-Zulu War, and though his injuries were serious enough to require surgery, a lengthy recovery, and using a cane, as far as I'm aware, he is not impotent. He, too, will be married next month, the same day as Spence," he huffed in frustration.

"But his injuries were not only physical," Harrison continued. He was revealing too much, but he trusted Francesca. "I observed the despair Tremain had sunk to. He needed to heal, and, to his credit, he accomplished it his way. You see, he studied for the church and has a divinity degree. Instead of joining the church after graduation, he chose to join the army."

The tale riveted Francesca; it was plain on her face. Yes, he no doubt revealed too much, but he entrusted her with keeping her word.

"He wished to give something back to humanity, serve his fellowman in a way that did not involve war and killing," Harrison continued. "I admire him for it. The family gave him the distance and time he requested to achieve those goals. Not only did it help thaw his frozen heart, as he called it, but it allowed a serene peace to enter his life—and a new spirituality. It opened his heart to love."

"This bit of gossip on your viscount brother originated from Lady Samantha Trimly by the by," Francesca interjected. "Vindictive piece of baggage. Also claimed your brother seduced a member of his congregation, a haughty governess of questionable background. The tale claims the lady of the house dismissed her for seducing one of her sons. I take it she is the woman he's to marry."

"Yes, she is." Harrison rolled his eyes.

Good God above.

Tremain's gossip traveled far and wide thanks to Lady Trimly, no doubt jealousy the main reason.

Eliza, Tremain's fiancée, could be considered haughty at the first meeting as her mode of speech was formal. Harrison surmised it was her upbringing in the orphanage and instruction by the nuns. But he soon concluded that Eliza possessed a generous, warm nature. Perfect for his brother.

"I feel rather cross now that I've repeated this malicious tittle-tattle; it put me right out of sorts," Francesca pouted teasingly.

"Then this should cheer you up." Harrison reached for a wooden satin-covered box and handed it to her. "Buttercreams from H.I. Rowntree and Company. I know you like them. They have begun to carry a new confection developed in Switzerland: milk chocolate."

Francesca squealed with delight as she adored chocolate. After opening the box, she peeled away the parchment paper. "Is it this lighter color, the milk chocolate?' she asked, her eyes sparkling.

"It is. Try it. I found it far sweeter than the dark one."

With a contented sigh, she bit into the small candy. "Delicious. I like the extra sweetness. Thank you, Tennington. You are thoughtful."

"Lift the tray," he coaxed in a soft voice.

She gave him a puzzled look but did as he asked. Her hand flew to her mouth to cover her gasp of shock. "Are they emeralds?"

"Yes, they are. I know you adore gold bracelets. Those tiny stones are emeralds."

Pulling it over her wrist, she gave him a radiant smile. "This is exquisite. I love it. Thank you, Tennington. I daresay this is almost as if this were a dismissal gift." Francesca's smile deflated. "Oh, this is goodbye. I had a feeling this was coming."

"There is more."

Francesca lifted the folded papers from the sweet box. She quickly scanned them. "You're giving me this house and the contents?" she whispered.

"Yes. It's yours to do as you will. It is not a large residence as town houses go. Live in the place, sell, or use it for your next affair, whatever you wish." He took her hand and kissed it. "It is goodbye, along with a heartfelt thank you. You kept up the pretense I was an unrepentant rake, and I appreciate the effort."

"I was a handy excuse and glad to maintain the illusion you kept me busy every night when in fact, you were not." She gave him a sad smile. "I will confess I'd hoped you would come more often. I truly did."

Harrison had other commitments—ones he would not reveal to Francesca, regardless of the trust between them.

She tapped the papers thoughtfully against her chin. "There will be no one else after you, Tennington. It's time to retire. I may be older than you think."

"Indeed? Care to elaborate?"

"I turned forty-two, three months past."

By God, she didn't look it.

"You are remarkably well-preserved," Harrison teased good-naturedly.

"It takes great care and effort to maintain such a state. It's time for Francesca Whitten to fade into the mist and for Annie Stokes to step forward. I think I will purchase a seaside cottage in a small village. Perhaps I'll meet a tall, broad-shouldered, handsome vicar much like your brother. My vicar will be distinguished, with a touch of gray at his temples. And will not care a whit for my past."

Harrison laughed. "You are a treasure, Francesca, or should I say—Annie?"

"That's my real name. You're the only one I've ever told."

He kissed her forehead, pushed the sheet away, and stood, looking for his clothes. Once he located them, he began to dress.

"You are a man of many secrets—a true puzzle. But I respect that you keep your covert life to yourself," she whispered.

A covert life. If she only knew.

"Look at me, Harry."

It was the first time she'd ever used his first name. He halted doing the buttons on his waistcoat and turned to face her.

Her expression was determined but laced with concern.

"If any man deserves true love, it is you, my dear. My severance package indicates that you will be shopping for a young lady of the aristocracy to be your bride—such a cold and loveless arrangement. I don't see that for you, Harry. I feel you will follow your brothers down the path of true love with a woman, not of your class."

She gave him a sad smile. "She may even be entirely inappropriate. If you meet such a lady, do not dismiss her. Nor dismiss what you feel. True love is rare, and many never experience it. Promise me you will give it a chance."

"Quite a speech. I have obligations—"

"Are your parents insisting you make an aristocratic match?" she asked.

"No, not at all."

"Then do not force the issue. Look by all means, but do not settle for anything less than true love. I'm giving advice and perhaps overstepping my boundaries, but it is kindly meant. I wish for you to be happy. As I said, you deserve love, and all it offers."

He nodded, too moved to speak. Blast it all; he didn't think his parting from Francesca—Annie—would affect him this deeply.

Clearing his throat, he said, "May you find all you desire, Annie."

"And you as well, my dear."

Slipping on his greatcoat and donning his hat, he exited the room and trotted down the stairs. Stepping into the night, he thought about her emotionally spoken words.

"I feel you will follow your brothers down the path of true love with a woman, not of your class. She may even be entirely inappropriate. If you meet such a lady, do not dismiss her. Nor dismiss what you feel."

He was the heir with an unspoken duty to marry well; because of it, he couldn't afford the luxury of loving someone not of his class.

It would be prudent to remember it.

www.ingramcontent.com/pod-product-compliance
Lightning Source LLC
Chambersburg PA
CBHW070115030726
47506CB00002B/750